The Plan Backfires

All morning long people had been talking about Sandra Ferris. Of course Jessica had explained to all her friends that the entire make-over was her idea. But no one seemed to care very much. They were much more interested in gossiping about the new Sandra—how pretty her hair looked, how boys who had never noticed her were stopping in the halls to talk to her.

Jessica felt left out. If it hadn't been for her, Sandra's make-over never would have happened. But Sandra wasn't telling anyone that. She was just lapping up all the attention. It wasn't fair!

Bantam Skylark Books in the SWEET VALLEY TWINS series
Ask your bookseller for the books you have missed

Sweet Valley Twins Super Editions

SWEET VALLEY TWINS

Jessica's Bad Idea

Written by
Jamie Suzanne

Created by
FRANCINE PASCAL

A BANTAM SKYLARK BOOK®
NEW YORK · TORONTO · LONDON · SYDNEY · AUCKLAND

RL 4, 008–012

JESSICA'S BAD IDEA
A Bantam Skylark Book / August 1989

*Sweet Valley High® and Sweet Valley Twins are
trademarks of Francine Pascal.*

Conceived by Francine Pascal

*Produced by Daniel Weiss Associates, Inc.,
27 West 20th Street, New York, NY 10011*

Cover art by James Mathewuse

*Skylark Books is a registered trademark of Bantam Books,
a division of Bantam Doubleday Dell Publishing Group, Inc.*

ISBN 0-553-15727-2

Published simultaneously in the United States and Canada

---

*Bantam Books are published by Bantam Books, a division of Bantam
Doubleday Dell Publishing Group, Inc. Its trademark, consisting of the
words "Bantam Books" and the portrayal of a rooster, is Registered in
U.S. Patent and Trademark Office and in other countries. Marca Regis-
trada. Bantam Books, 666 Fifth Avenue, New York, New York 10103.*

PRINTED IN THE UNITED STATES OF AMERICA

OPM   0 9 8 7 6 5 4 3 2 1

Jessica's
Bad Idea

One

◇

"Coming to you, Jess," Elizabeth Wakefield called, passing the volleyball in a perfect arc to her twin sister, Jessica.

It was a sunny Monday morning, and the twins' gym class at Sweet Valley Middle School was playing volleyball outside.

Jessica leaped high in the air, just in time to meet Elizabeth's setup. She drove the ball down over the net. Two girls on the other team tried to hit it back, but they both missed. "All right!" cried Jessica. She and Elizabeth slapped hands, and the rest of their teammates cheered.

Mrs. Langberg, the twins' gym teacher, blew her whistle for silence. "Good play," she said. She glanced at her watch. "I'm afraid that's all we have time for this morning. Class dismissed."

Jessica and Elizabeth trotted into the locker room and began changing from their blue gym uniforms into their school clothes. All around them, the other girls were doing the same.

"These uniforms are so boring," Jessica groaned as she studied herself in the mirror. "I wish we could wear something more exciting."

"I don't think Mrs. Langberg would go for that," Elizabeth replied. "Remember what she said the day Ellen Riteman came to class in purple sweats?" She imitated Mrs. Langberg's stern voice. " 'This is a gym class, young lady, not a fashion show!' "

"I know, I know," Jessica said. "But I wonder if she'd mind if I just spruced up my uniform a little? Maybe I could sew some gold spangles down the sides."

Elizabeth laughed. "Whatever gave you an idea like that, Jess?"

"Oh, I have lots of fashion ideas. Plenty of them are just as good as the ones in fashion magazines, too."

"Well, unless you want Mrs. Langberg to blow her top," Elizabeth warned, "you'd better leave your uniform just the way it is."

"Oh, all right." Jessica sighed. She untied her ponytail and began combing out her hair.

Looking at the twins was almost like seeing double. Both girls had blond, silky hair, sparkling blue-green eyes, and a dimple in their left cheeks when they smiled. But their family and friends knew that was where the similarities ended.

Elizabeth was the older of the two—by four minutes, though it sometimes seemed more like four years. She was very committed to *The Sweet Valley Sixers*, the sixth-grade newspaper she had helped to start, and she hoped that someday she would become a professional journalist. She also made time for her friends and family, and occasionally she spent time alone, curled up with a good book.

Jessica, on the other hand, was never seen without a group of girls around her. She was a member of the Unicorn Club, an exclusive group of the most popular girls at Sweet Valley Middle School. They were all her best friends. They spent most of their time discussing boys, fashions, and soap operas. Elizabeth usually referred to the Unicorns as the "snob squad." But in spite of their differences, Jessica and Elizabeth were still best friends, and they would do anything for each other.

When the twins finished dressing, they grabbed their books and left the locker room. "Hey, wait up!" Kerry Glenn called, running after them.

"Hi, Kerry," Elizabeth said. "What's up?"

"I wanted to tell you about my birthday party," Kerry replied, tucking a strand of her hair behind her ear. "It's this Saturday, and you're both invited. I sent out the invitations over the weekend."

"It sounds great! Who else is coming?" Jessica asked with interest.

"Everybody. I invited the whole ballet class. And lots of girls from school, too. Oh," Kerry added glumly, "and Sandra Ferris."

"Sandra Ferris?" Jessica repeated, making a face. "Why did you invite her?"

"My mother told me I had to. She's a friend of Sandra's mom, so she said I had to ask her."

"But Sandra's so weird," Jessica moaned. "And she's such a klutz. She's always tripping over her feet."

"Yeah." Kerry sighed. "I wish I didn't have to invite her."

"Hey, don't be so mean," Elizabeth said. "Sandra's shy, but that doesn't mean she's not a nice person."

"How do you know?" Kerry asked. "Are you her friend?"

"Well, not exactly, but we used to be friends back in elementary school. I'm not sure what happened. I guess we just got interested in different things."

"Then she went to another school for a couple of years, didn't she?" Jessica added.

"I think so," Elizabeth said. "Anyway, Sandra can't be half as bad as you're making her sound."

"She's worse!" Jessica exclaimed.

"Jessica's right," Kerry nodded. "Sandra Ferris is a total loser."

Just then the next period bell rang. "It's going to be a great party, anyway," Kerry said as she hurried into her math class. "I hope you can both come."

"We'll be there," Elizabeth promised, waving to her friend.

When school ended, Jessica and Elizabeth hopped on their bicycles and headed toward home. "Come on," Jessica called. "I'll race you to the house."

Jessica took off down the street with Elizabeth close behind. By the time they reached their driveway, they were practically side by side.

Jessica skidded into the driveway and leapt off her bike. "I won!" she cried triumphantly.

"You started before me," Elizabeth protested. When she looked at her sister's face, she had to smile. "OK, you did win," she admitted.

When Jessica and Elizabeth let themselves in through the kitchen door, they were greeted by their fourteen-year-old brother, Steven. He was in his usual spot at the counter, devouring a plate of home-baked chocolate chip cookies.

"Hey, hold on!" Jessica cried, running toward him. "Save some for us."

"Were you planning to eat all these by yourself?" Elizabeth demanded, grabbing a cookie.

"Who, me?" Steven asked innocently.

The twins looked at each other and rolled their eyes. Sometimes Steven could be such a pain!

They were just about to sit down and dig into the cookies when the phone rang. "I'll get it," Jessica said. She popped one of the cookies into her mouth and ran to answer the phone. It was Lila Fowler, her best friend from the Unicorn Club.

"I got an invitation in the mail to Kerry Glenn's birthday party," Lila said. "Were you invited, too?"

"Yes," Jessica said. "Have you thought about a present yet?"

"Not really," Lila replied. "Kerry likes ballet, doesn't she?"

"Definitely. She never misses a lesson."

"Well, I saw a ballerina music box at the mall. Maybe I'll buy her that."

Jessica tried to think of something interesting she could buy. Then suddenly she had an idea. "Since Kerry loves ballet," she exclaimed, "let's tell everybody who was invited to bring presents with a ballet theme."

"Jess, what a great idea!" Lila agreed.

After Jessica hung up, she ran back into the kitchen to share her idea with her sister.

"A ballet theme party!" Elizabeth cried. "Jess, that's perfect!"

"I'll call Kerry's mother tonight and find out who's coming to the party," Jessica said. "Then I'll call the girls and tell them all to bring ballet presents."

"Do you want some help with the phone calls?" Elizabeth asked. "It sounds like a lot of work."

Normally, Jessica was more than happy to share her work with Elizabeth. But giving ballet presents to Kerry was her idea, and she wanted to spread the news herself. "Thanks," she said, "but I don't mind."

"OK, just remember to call everybody." She glanced at Jessica and added, "Including Sandra Ferris."

Jessica groaned. Sometimes she thought Elizabeth was too nice for her own good.

After dinner, Jessica called Kerry's mother and explained her idea about the ballet theme presents. Mrs. Glenn was delighted. She gave Jessica the names and phone numbers of all the girls who were invited to Kerry's party.

There were twenty names on the list. Jessica stretched out on the living room sofa and started dialing. All the girls she talked to loved her idea. Melissa McCormick said she'd seen a pair of turquoise ballet slippers at the mall that would be perfect for Kerry. Grace Oliver knew a store where she could buy a set of barrettes decorated with ballerinas. And Olivia Davidson planned to buy Kerry a book about Mikhail Baryshnikov.

After the tenth phone call, Jessica closed her eyes and sighed. She didn't feel like making any more calls. The novelty had worn off and now she was bored. She thought about what she would wear to school tomorrow. Members of the Unicorn Club tried to wear at least one purple thing every day. She decided to head upstairs and look through her closet, when she remembered that she still had calls to make.

Then she had an idea. She would see most of the girls in school tomorrow, and she could talk to them then. In any case, the girls she had already called would probably spread the word. And she could always make the rest of the calls tomorrow night.

Two

◇

Sandra Ferris sang "Happy Birthday" along with the other girls, but her heart wasn't in it. Instead of being happy, she felt like an outcast. Kerry's birthday party had been going on for almost an hour now, but not one of the girls had said more than two words to her. Even Kerry was ignoring her.

Sandra was sure she knew why. She wasn't pretty, popular, and talented like the other girls. She was tall, awkward, and shy.

While the girls sang, Kerry's mother walked into the room carrying a huge chocolate cake. There were plastic ballerinas dancing across the top and flaming candles surrounding them. As the singing ended, she placed the cake on the table in front of Kerry.

"Make a wish, Kerry!" Mrs. Glenn urged.

"Wish for something exciting," Jessica Wakefield added.

Kerry closed her eyes. Then she took a deep breath and blew out all the candles. The girls cheered loudly.

After all the cake and ice cream were gone, the girls moved into the family room to watch Kerry open her presents. Sandra sat a little apart from everyone else. Even so, she could still hear Kimberly Haver and Jessica Wakefield whispering about her.

"Who invited *her*?" Kimberly asked.

"Who?" Jessica replied.

"You know. *Her*. The giraffe."

Jessica glanced at Sandra and giggled. "Look at her. Even sitting down she's about a foot taller than anyone else in the room!"

Sandra looked at Jessica and Kimberly and sighed. Both girls were so pretty. Sandra, on the other hand, felt plain, right down to her brown, frizzy hair.

I feel like an ugly duckling in a roomful of swans, she thought sadly.

"Hi, Sandra."

Sandra turned to see Elizabeth Wakefield sitting down beside her. "Oh, hi, Elizabeth," she said shyly.

"This is a great party, isn't it?"

"I guess so," Sandra said. And then she added softly, "But I don't think I belong here."

"Why not?" Elizabeth asked.

Sandra shrugged. "I just don't fit in."

"Sandra, that's not true!" Elizabeth exclaimed.

But before she could say anything else, Kerry announced, "This first present is from Sarah Thomas." She ripped off the wrapping paper and pulled out a beautiful pink leotard. "Oh, Sarah," she cried, "it's gorgeous! Thanks!"

The next present she opened was from Kimberly Haver. It was a pair of pale blue tights. "These will look terrific with the leotard," Kerry said happily.

Kerry opened three more gifts. All of them had something to do with ballet. Then Kerry picked up Sandra's present. Sandra's big sister had helped her pick it out. It was a pair of soft brown leather gloves, perfect for those few winter days when the weather in Sweet Valley was rainy and chilly.

Kerry opened the box and pulled out the gloves. Suddenly, the room fell silent. Everybody watched as Kerry tried them on. They looked silly next to her red party dress. Plus, they were too big.

"Gee, thanks, Sandra," Kerry said, but she didn't sound like she meant it. She took off the gloves and tossed them aside. A couple of the girls giggled.

Then Kimberly leaned over to Jessica and said in a loud whisper, "What's the matter with her? Everybody knows we were supposed to bring presents that had something to do with ballet."

Jessica just shrugged and rolled her eyes.

Sandra was so embarrassed she wanted to die. Everyone had bought Kerry a ballet present—everyone except her. No wonder they were giggling.

Hot tears filled Sandra's eyes. In a moment they would spill over and fall down her cheeks. She had to get out of there before anyone saw her crying. She just had to!

Sandra jumped to her feet. "Excuse me," she mumbled. "I . . . I have to find the bathroom." Before anyone could say a word, she ran out of the room. She had no idea where she was going. All she knew was she had to get away from the whispers and giggles of the other girls.

She stumbled down the hall and stopped at the first room she saw. It was a study, filled with books and a big desk. The room was empty, so she hurried inside and shut the door behind her. Then she fell into a chair and burst into tears.

Suddenly, there was a knock at the door. Sandra looked up and wiped her eyes. "Who is it?" she asked.

"It's Elizabeth," the voice said. "Can I come in?"

"Go away." Sandra sniffled. "Just leave me alone."

"Please?" Elizabeth opened the door a crack and looked in. "I just want to talk. OK?"

"There's nothing to talk about. I never should have come. I don't belong at this party."

"You do, too," Elizabeth cried. She walked into the room and shut the door behind her. "What's wrong, Sandra? Why did you run out of the room?"

"Didn't you hear the other girls laughing at me?" Sandra felt hot with embarrassment. "I'm the only one who didn't know to bring a ballet present."

"That was Jessica's idea," Elizabeth explained. "Didn't she tell you? She called all the girls to tell them about it."

"Well, she didn't call me," Sandra said.

"She didn't? But she promised me she would!"

"Don't blame your sister," Sandra said. "I was only invited to this party because Kerry's mother made her ask me. Kerry's not my friend and I don't fit in with anyone here."

"What do you mean? You're no different from the rest of us."

Sandra felt the tears starting again. "But I am," she insisted. "Just look at me."

Elizabeth sat on the edge of the desk. "Here," she said handing Sandra a tissue. "Now, tell me why you think you don't fit in."

Sandra hesitated. She and Elizabeth had been

friends once, but that was a long time ago. Since then, Elizabeth had become one of the most popular girls at school. Still, she seemed just as friendly and nice as always.

"Oh, I don't know," Sandra began. She shrugged. "I've never been pretty like you. But this year has been the worst ever. For starters, I grew four inches over the summer." She stretched out her long legs. "Just look at me. I look like a stork!"

"Four inches!" Elizabeth exclaimed. "That must be hard to get used to."

"It is. I was never graceful, but now I feel like I have two left feet. I'm always tripping over something or banging into someone. It's awful."

"Being tall isn't all bad," Elizabeth protested. "It helps when you play volleyball and basketball. Plus, you can reach things other people can't. And besides, all the most famous fashion models are tall."

Sandra laughed. "Yeah, and beautiful. I could never be a model. Never in a million years."

"You never know," Elizabeth said. Then she smiled. "Sandra, what are you doing tomorrow?"

"I don't know." Sandra sniffed. "Why?"

"I just thought you might like to go bike riding with me. And then you could eat dinner at my house."

Sandra could hardly believe her ears. Elizabeth Wakefield wanted to go bike riding with her! But then her face fell. "You're just being nice because you feel sorry for me," she said glumly.

"I am not. I'm being nice because I like you. Now, come on. Do you want to go bike riding or don't you?"

Sandra smiled. "OK. I'd like that."

Elizabeth jumped up and grabbed Sandra's hand. "Good. Now let's get back to the party. Kerry's mother rented a video of *The Red Shoes*."

"Oh, Elizabeth, I can't go back in there and face those girls. I'm too embarrassed."

"Yes, you can," Elizabeth insisted. "Just hold your head up and ignore them. Besides, you don't want to miss *The Red Shoes*, do you? It's the best ballet movie ever."

Sandra sighed. "Well . . . all right. But can I sit with you?"

"Of course you can. Now, let's go."

Sandra followed Elizabeth down the hall to the family room. The girls were already watching the movie when Sandra walked back into the room. A few girls turned and stared. Sandra heard whispers and giggles. She knew they were meant for her, but she remembered what Elizabeth had told her to do. She took a deep breath, held up her head, crossed the room, and sat down on the floor. Elizabeth sat down next to her and together the two girls watched *The Red Shoes*.

* * *

When the party ended, Mrs. Wakefield picked up the twins in the family's maroon van.

As soon as the girls got in, Elizabeth turned to her sister. "Jessica, how *could* you?" she demanded.

"How could I what?"

"You know what I'm talking about. You promised me you'd call all the girls who were invited to Kerry's party. *All* of them. Including Sandra."

"I know, Lizzie," Jessica said, "but I got busy. There were tons of girls invited to that party, you know. And Sandra wasn't the only one I didn't get to call."

"Then why was Sandra the only one who didn't bring a ballet present?" Elizabeth asked.

"Because she's a nerd!"

"Jessica," Mrs. Wakefield interrupted, "please don't talk like that."

"But, Mom," Jessica insisted, "all the other girls found out about the ballet theme from talking to their friends. Can I help it if Sandra doesn't have any friends?"

"Well, she's got one now," Elizabeth said. "I invited her to go bike riding with me tomorrow afternoon. And, Mom, can Sandra stay for dinner?"

"Why, of course," Mrs. Wakefield said with a smile. She drove the van into the Wakefields' driveway.

Elizabeth turned to her sister. "Why don't you come bike riding with us tomorrow? Who knows? You might find out you actually like Sandra."

Jessica frowned. "Look, if you want to be friends with Sandra Ferris, go ahead," she said grumpily. "But don't expect *me* to be nice to her!" With that she jumped out of the van and ran into the house.

Three

◇

"Ouch!" Jessica cried. She was trying to sew a lace collar onto one of her angora sweaters, but she was failing miserably. Her fingertip was starting to look like a pin cushion!

Jessica heard the sound of laughter. It was Elizabeth and Sandra Ferris doing their homework together in Elizabeth's room. Jessica frowned. Ever since Kerry Glenn's birthday party, Elizabeth and Sandra had been spending time together. On Sunday they went bike riding, and on Monday they ate lunch together with Elizabeth's friends, Amy Sutton and Julie Porter. Now it was Tuesday, and Elizabeth had brought Sandra home from school with her.

"Hi, Jessica!"

Jessica looked up to see Sandra standing at her bedroom door. "Don't you believe in knocking?" Jessica demanded.

"Oh I'm sorry," Sandra appologized. "Elizabeth said to tell you we're going to the mall. She was wondering if you wanted to come along."

With you? Jessica thought. *Fat chance*. Out loud she said, "No. I'm busy."

"Oh," Sandra looked curiously at Jessica's sewing. "What are you making?" she asked.

"It's a fashion idea I had," Jessica said proudly. "I found these antique lace cuffs and collar in a thrift store downtown. I'm sewing them onto my sweater."

"That's going to look so pretty!" Sandra walked over to the bed and looked at Jessica's sewing. "I could never come up with an idea like that."

"Oh, I have tons of ideas," Jessica replied. "I make drawings of all my designs. Someday, I'll probably be a famous fashion designer."

Sandra picked up Jessica's sweater and looked at the collar. "What kind of stitch are you using?" she asked.

"I don't know. Just a regular one, I guess."

"This looks like a basting stitch. You should try making the stitches tighter and closer together. Otherwise it might not hold."

Jessica didn't want advice from Sandra. "I know what I'm doing," she said irritably.

"I'm sorry," Sandra said shyly and then asked, "Jessica, can I look at some of your designs?"

So far, Jessica hadn't shown her designs to anyone except Elizabeth. She was afraid no one would like them. But Sandra was different—Jessica felt sure she could impress *her*. "OK," she said. She pointed to a drawing pad on her cluttered desk. "They're in that pad."

Sandra picked up the pad and leafed through it. There was a picture of purple cotton pants with elastic at the ankles and one of a blue gym uniform with spangles, plus a dozen other designs.

"These are terrific!" Sandra exclaimed. She closed the drawing pad. "I wish I knew as much about fashion as you do," she said admiringly. "I mean, you always know just what to wear."

"It's not so difficult," Jessica said modestly. "Anyone can buy pretty clothes."

"But it's not just your clothes," Sandra insisted. "It's the way you put things together. And the way you wear your hair. You know so much about looking good."

Jessica was flattered. "I guess I am pretty good at that kind of thing. But any girl can look nice if she tries. It's just a matter of finding the right hairstyle, the right clothes—"

"Any girl except me," Sandra said glumly. "I

mean, just look at me. I'm too tall, I'm too skinny. My hair is a mess. My ears stick out—"

"Hold on," Jessica interrupted. "There's nothing wrong with being tall and thin. And you could wear your hair differently." She jumped up and pushed Sandra's hair away from her face. "Yes, that's it." She nodded approvingly. "That looks better."

"It does?" Sandra asked uncertainly.

"Of course it does. But just changing your hair isn't enough. What you need is a complete make-over—hair, clothes, everything."

"Do you really think it would help?" Sandra asked.

"Sure it would. You need to learn how to let your good points show."

Sandra bit her lip. "Jessica," she asked shyly, "would . . . would you teach me?"

Jessica paused for a moment. Could she possibly transform Sandra the Plain into Sandra the Beautiful? She could at least turn her into a less embarrassing friend for Elizabeth. Besides, she had never done a complete make-over before. It might be fun. "Sure," she said finally, with a shrug. "Why not?"

"Oh, I can't believe it!" Sandra cried. Then she ran to tell Elizabeth.

When Elizabeth heard about the make-over, she

was thrilled. "That sounds like more fun than going to the mall," she said with enthusiasm.

With Jessica giving the orders, the twins set to work. First they washed Sandra's hair and used a creme rinse to make it soft and full. Then they styled it in a French braid with wispy bangs. Finally, Jessica rubbed a soft blusher into Sandra's cheeks and gave her lips a light coat of pink lip gloss.

Next came the clothes. Sandra was wearing faded jeans and a baggy green T-shirt. Jessica made her change into one of Elizabeth's blouses—a white sleeveless one with a scooped neck. Jessica donated her braided purple belt for Sandra to wear. And Elizabeth lent her a slender silver horse pendant.

When they were all finished, Jessica placed a mirror in Sandra's hand. "Well," Jessica asked, "what do you think?"

Sandra held the mirror up to her face. The girl who looked back at her was very, very pretty. Sandra could hardly believe her eyes! For a full minute she just stared at herself. "Is that really me?" she gasped at last.

"It sure is," Elizabeth said.

Sandra shook her head. "I just can't believe it!" she exclaimed.

"But that's only the beginning," Jessica said.

"There's more?" Sandra asked with surprise.

"You said you wanted a complete make-over. Well, looking pretty is only part of it." Jessica sat on her bed and gazed at Sandra critically. "OK, let me see you walk."

Sandra shuffled across the room. Her shoulders were slumped and her head was down.

"No, no!" Jessica cried. "Shoulders back! Head up!"

"You sound like a drill sergeant," Elizabeth said, giggling.

"Well, I can't help it," Jessica said. She grabbed her math book from her desk. "Here, Sandra. Balance this on your head while you walk. And when you talk to me, keep your head up and look me straight in the eye."

Jessica and Elizabeth spent the next half hour teaching Sandra how to walk, talk, and smile with confidence. Finally, Jessica was satisfied. "You're doing great," she told Sandra. "Now let's go for a walk and try out your new look on the world."

"What?" Sandra gasped. "Oh, no, I can't do that!"

"Of course you can," Elizabeth said. "We'll just go around the block."

"Well, if you say so. But do you really think I'm ready?"

"Sure," Elizabeth said. "Come on."

Jessica, Elizabeth, and Sandra left the house and

started down the sidewalk. They had barely gone a block when they saw some kids from school riding their bikes toward them. It was Ricky Capaldo, Aaron Dallas, and Tom McKay—three boys who always made a point of teasing Sandra.

"Oh, no," Sandra moaned. "They're going to laugh when they see me."

"Relax," Jessica whispered. "Just keep your head up and smile."

Sandra did as she was told. The boys pedaled past. "Hi, Elizabeth! Hi, Jessica!" they called.

Then suddenly, Ricky Capaldo slammed on his brakes. "Hey," he cried, "is that you, Sandra?"

Sandra turned and smiled nervously. "Hi, Ricky."

Aaron and Tom stopped pedaling. "Wow!" exclaimed Tom. "It *is* Sandra!"

"You sure look different," Aaron added.

Sandra giggled. "I do?"

"Yeah!" Ricky exclaimed. "It sure is an improvement!"

Sandra was beaming. "Gee, thanks."

The boys rode away, still shaking their heads over the "new" Sandra Ferris. "I think your new look is a hit," Elizabeth said with a smile.

The girls walked the rest of the way around the block and then headed back to the Wakefields' house. When they returned, they found Steven in the front yard, sweeping dirt off the driveway. Usually, Steven ignored the twins and their friends. But now he leaned on his broom and smiled. "Hi there, girls."

"Uh-oh," Jessica said, "Steven's being nice. He must want a favor."

"Can't a brother just be nice to his sisters?" Steven asked. He glanced at Sandra. "Who's your friend?"

"Don't you remember Sandra Ferris?" Jessica asked. "She ate dinner with us on Sunday."

Steven took a closer look. "Hey, you're right! Boy, do you look different!"

"We gave Sandra a complete make-over," Jessica said proudly. "What do you think?"

"Wow!" Steven exclaimed. He smiled at Sandra. They were almost the same height. "Hey, Sandra, I was just wondering," he said suddenly. "Do you play basketball?"

"Sometimes," Sandra said shyly. "I'm better at volleyball, though."

"Oh, yeah? I play volleyball at the beach. There's always a pickup game on Saturdays. Do you ever play there?"

"No," Sandra said. "I never have."

"Well, you should." He shrugged and added quickly, "I mean, you know, if you're not too busy." Steven grinned nervously. Then he picked up his broom and hurried off into the garage.

The girls looked at each other. "Did you see that?" Jessica asked her twin in amazement.

"I've never seen Steven so tongue-tied," Elizabeth laughed.

Sandra didn't know what to think. She felt like a character in a fairy tale. Just a couple of hours ago she'd been a nobody. Now suddenly everyone was treating her like a beautiful princess. It was crazy and a little scary. But most of all, it was fun.

"Tomorrow the whole school will see the new Sandra," Jessica said. "What are you planning to wear?"

"Gee, I don't know," Sandra answered. "I don't have anything really special. Besides, I outgrew practically all my clothes over the summer."

"I have an idea," Elizabeth said. "Let's ask Mom if you can stay for dinner. Then later we can go over to the mall and go shopping."

"I just got my allowance yesterday," Sandra said eagerly. "Maybe I'll find something on sale."

"If not, you can borrow something of ours," Elizabeth suggested.

"Come on," Jessica said impatiently, "we've got a lot of planning to do." She linked arms with Sandra and Elizabeth, and together the three girls hurried into the house.

Four

◇

"What do you think, Lizzie?" Jessica asked, as the twins walked to school the next morning. She twirled around, showing off her angora sweater with the new lace collar and cuffs. "Doesn't it look good?"

"It's beautiful," Elizabeth said. "But the cuffs look a little loose. Are you sure you sewed them on tightly enough?"

"Of course I did." Actually, Jessica wasn't sure. She had been so busy with Sandra's make-over that she hadn't had a moment to think about her sewing. It was only this morning, before breakfast, that she had quickly finished sewing on the cuffs. *Oh, well, as long as it looks good*, she told herself, *that's all that really matters*.

When the girls reached Sweet Valley Middle School, they saw Amy Sutton and Julie Porter hurrying across the grassy lawn to meet them.

"Have you heard the news?" Julie said breathlessly. "Sandra Ferris looks like a new person. She changed her hair, her clothes, everything. She's even wearing makeup!"

"Everybody's talking about it," Amy added. "She looks great!"

"Look," Julie whispered, "there she is now!"

Sandra was walking across the lawn toward them. She was wearing a faded denim blouse and a pair of tan stonewashed jeans. She had her shoulders back and her head held high, just the way Jessica had taught her. As she walked, every person she passed turned to look at her.

"How did she get her hair to look so soft and full?" Amy wondered. She twisted a strand of her own limp blond hair. "I'd like to know her secret."

"Sandra," Elizabeth called, "over here!"

Sandra walked over and joined her friends. "Hi," she said with a shy smile.

"You look fabulous!" Julie cried.

"I love your hair," Amy added.

"Thanks," Sandra said, smiling with pleasure.

"That outfit is fantastic," Julie said. "Where did you get it?"

"I bought the blouse yesterday at the mall," Sandra answered.

"I lent her the jeans," Jessica broke in. "You see, yesterday after school Sandra came over to visit Elizabeth and—"

But before Jessica could explain, Ricky Capaldo walked by with Tom Sleeter, the vice-president of the student council. "See, I told you," Ricky was saying.

"Wow, you weren't kidding!" Tom gasped, looking in Sandra's direction.

"Yo, Sandra," Ricky called. "What's happening?"

"Hi, Sandra," Tom said with a wave.

Sandra blushed pink. "Hello," she said shyly.

"Wow," Elizabeth said, turning her attention back to Sandra. "You're all anyone is talking about."

"Well, you deserve the attention," Julie said to Sandra. "You look great!"

Jessica frowned. Everyone was paying so much attention to Sandra, they hadn't even noticed her sweater with the beautiful new lace collar and cuffs. And what was the matter with Sandra anyway? She was acting as if she had thought up her new look all by herself. Why didn't she tell everyone that Jessica had given her the make-over?

Just then Jessica noticed Lila Fowler and some of

the other Unicorns standing by the fountain, talking excitedly. She was sure *they* would notice her new sweater. "See you later," she said to Elizabeth. She hurried across the lawn to join the Unicorns. When she reached the fountain she struck a graceful pose and waited for everyone to notice her. Finally, they did, but their reaction wasn't what she expected.

"Jessica," Lila said eagerly, "have you seen Sandra Ferris?"

Jessica started to answer, but Janet Howell cut her off.

"Can you believe it?" Janet exclaimed. "She actually looks good!"

"Did you see Tom Sleeter looking at her?" Ellen Riteman asked.

"How could you miss it?" Lila giggled.

"He's cute," Janet said.

"I hate to admit it, but Sandra is, too," Ellen said with amazement.

Jessica felt like a balloon that had just had all the air let out of it. Not even her closest friends had noticed her sweater. But they were sure to be impressed when she told them she was the one who had given Sandra the new look. "Sandra was over at my house yesterday after school," she began. "I showed her—"

"She's friends with your sister, isn't she?" Janet interrupted.

But before Jessica could answer, the bell rang.

"Oops, I've got to hurry," Lila cried. "I have a whole page of math problems to do before first period."

"I need to take these books back to the library," Ellen said. "They're two days overdue."

The girls hurried into the school. With a frustrated sigh, Jessica picked up her books and followed.

When the lunch bell rang later that day, Jessica left her classroom and walked down the hall with a frown on her face. All morning long people had been talking about Sandra Ferris. Of course Jessica had explained to all her friends that the entire make-over was her idea. But no one seemed to care very much. They were more interested in gossiping about the new Sandra—how pretty her hair looked, how she didn't seem quite so awkward anymore, how boys who had never noticed her were stopping in the halls to talk to her.

Jessica felt left out. If it hadn't been for her, Sandra's make-over never would have happened. But Sandra wasn't telling anyone that. She was just lapping up all the attention. It wasn't fair!

Jessica walked into the cafeteria, grabbed some lunch, and walked toward the table where the Unicorns always sat. But today someone else was sitting with them—Sandra Ferris!

"Hi, Jessica," Sandra said with a smile. "Come sit next to me."

"We were just asking Sandra about her make-over," Lila explained to Jessica.

"Where did you get that pretty blouse?" Janet asked Sandra.

"I bought it at the mall last night," she answered. "At Valley Fashions."

"I helped her pick it out," Jessica interrupted. She put her lunch tray on the table and sat down. "I knew it would go with the jeans I lent her." But no one was even listening to Jessica.

"Did they have any others?" Ellen Riteman asked. "I'd love to get one."

Suddenly, out of the corner of her eye, Jessica noticed Caroline Pearce rushing across the cafeteria toward the Unicorn table. Caroline was the biggest gossip in the whole school. Nothing made her happier than spreading a big, juicy rumor—even if it wasn't one hundred percent true.

Normally, Jessica thought Caroline's prissy know-it-all attitude was a big pain. But today she welcomed anything that would take everyone's mind off Sandra Ferris. "Hi, Caroline," Jessica called loudly. "What's new?"

"Have you heard?" Caroline said breathlessly. She plopped down at the end of the Unicorn table, obviously waiting for the suspense to build.

"Heard what?" Janet asked at last.

"A group of East German gymnasts are coming to visit Sweet Valley soon," she announced. "They're all kids our age and they're going to stay with local families."

"Really?" Sandra exclaimed. "That sounds exciting!"

"How did you hear about it?" Janet asked.

"My mother is on the welcoming committee," Caroline said proudly.

"Do you know the names of the gymnasts?" Ellen asked. "Are they famous?"

"I don't know yet," Caroline answered. "But they must be famous if the East German government is sending them to the United States." With that, she jumped up and hurried off to spread the news to another table.

Jessica and her friends couldn't stop talking about the East German gymnasts. Would they all be girls, or would there be boys, too? Would the gymnasts put on an exhibition at the middle school? And most important of all, would the Unicorns get to meet them?

The girls were still talking when Bruce Patman walked up. Bruce was a seventh grader and just about the cutest boy in the whole school. "Hi, Jessica," he said. "Hi, Janet, Lila, Ellen." He turned to Sandra. "And who's this? Christie Brinkley?"

Sandra giggled and her cheeks turned a soft shade of pink. "No."

Suddenly, no one at the Unicorn table was thinking about gymnastics. Everyone was much more interested in seeing what was happening between Bruce and Sandra.

"Oh, excuse me," Bruce went on. "My mistake. You're Cybill Shepherd, right?"

Sandra giggled again and lowered her eyes. "Stop teasing," she said.

"OK, here's the truth. You're the girl who's going to share her brownie with me." Bruce grabbed the brownie from Sandra's tray and took a huge bite.

"Hey, give that back!" Sandra cried. Bruce held the brownie over her head. She reached up to grab it, but he whisked it behind his back. "Bru-uce!" Sandra cried with frustration.

Bruce grinned and handed the brownie back to Sandra. "Sweets for the sweet," he said. Then he walked away.

"Gosh," Lila said when Bruce was gone, "I think he likes you, Sandra."

Sandra shook her head. "No, not Bruce Patman. He'd never look twice at a girl like me."

"But he just did," Lila insisted.

"Lila's right," Tamara Chase pointed out. "He only teases girls he really likes."

Bruce Patman flirting with Sandra Ferris! The

thought made Jessica hot with jealousy. All her angry feelings from the morning flooded back. "I think he's just making fun of you, Sandra," she said meanly.

Then suddenly, Lila laughed loudly.

"What's so funny?" Jessica demanded.

Lila pointed at Jessica's sleeve. "I think you're losing something."

Jessica looked down. One of the new lace cuffs had fallen off her sweater and was lying in her plate of macaroni and cheese!

The whole table burst out laughing. Sandra was laughing, too. "I told you to use tighter stitches," she said with a giggle.

Jessica could feel her face turning red. She'd never felt so humiliated in her whole life. She glared at Sandra as she yanked the lace cuff out of the macaroni and cheese. "I don't think Bruce Patman likes you, Sandra," she said angrily. "And I *know* I don't!" Then she jumped up from the table and ran out of the cafeteria.

Five

◇

The next day, the kids at Sweet Valley Middle School were still talking about Sandra's new look. Teachers complimented her, and boys who had barely noticed her before stopped in the halls to talk. Everybody wanted to get close and take a look.

Sandra walked around in a state of shock. She felt sure she must be dreaming. Any minute she would wake up and discover she was still clumsy and unpopular. But to her amazement, things kept getting better and better.

That day in home economics, the class broke into groups to learn how to make an omelette. Normally, no one wanted to work with Sandra. In fact, Mrs.

Gerhart usually had to assign her to one of the groups.

But today, Julie Porter and Kerry Glenn actually asked Sandra to cook with them. And even when Sandra accidentally knocked a pan off the counter with her elbow, Julie and Kerry didn't make fun of her. That made Sandra so happy, she forgot to feel embarrassed. In fact, she felt great.

Sandra's next class was gym. Mrs. Langberg took the class outside to play coed volleyball. Sandra liked volleyball, but usually she was so afraid of making a bad play that she didn't try anything fancy. Today, however, she was feeling more confident. She stood at the net, waiting for the ball to come to her. When it finally did, she heard her teammates behind her screaming, "Spike it, Sandra! Spike it!"

Sandra leaped high in the air and hit the ball with all her might. It flew across the net and landed in the grass with a thud. A perfect spike!

"Way to go, Sandra!" her teammates cheered. Sandra just grinned. She felt terrific!

That afternoon, Jessica walked to social studies class alone. All the talk about Sandra's new look was really getting on her nerves. Sure, it was nice to know she had done such a good job with the make-over. But why was everyone paying so much attention to Sandra and so little to her? It just wasn't fair.

*If I never hear another word about Sandra Ferris it will
be too soon!* she thought grumpily. Just then she saw
Caroline Pearce hurrying toward her.

"Jessica, have you heard?" Caroline began.

"Heard what?" Jessica snapped. "That Sandra's
make-over was all my idea?"

"That's old news. The latest is that Janet Howell
wants Sandra to join the Unicorns."

Jessica's mouth fell open. "I don't believe it!" she
gasped. But Caroline had already rushed off to tell
the news to someone else.

Jessica walked into social studies and sat down.
She knew that half the time Caroline's gossip turned
out to be at least partly untrue. But what if this time
she was right? The thought made her angry. Sandra
Ferris wasn't special like the rest of the Unicorns.
Why, if it weren't for me, Jessica told herself, *Sandra
would still be a complete nobody!*

Just then Elizabeth and Sandra walked into the
room together. Elizabeth sat down next to her twin.
"Is something wrong, Jess? You look like you just
lost your best friend."

But before Jessica could answer, their teacher, Mrs.
Arnette, rapped on her desk. "As you all know," she
began, "next weekend our town celebrates Sweet
Valley Days. During that time we honor the early
settlers of our town. Now, can anyone tell me when
Sweet Valley was founded?"

"I didn't know it was lost!" Jim Sturbridge shouted. The class burst out laughing.

"That's quite enough, Jim," Mrs. Arnette said sternly. She patted her hairnet and peered over her glasses. "Anyone else?"

Jessica raised her hand. "Was it 1492?" she asked.

Mrs. Arnette frowned. "Hardly! That was the year Columbus discovered the New World. Now, do we have any reasonable answers?"

Slowly, Sandra Ferris raised her hand. Jessica stared in amazement. She couldn't believe what she was seeing. Sandra hardly ever said a word in class, even when she was called on.

"Ah, Sandra," Mrs. Arnette said, "how nice to see you raising your hand. Do you know when Sweet Valley was founded?"

"The first Spanish settlers arrived in this area in 1788," Sandra explained, "but Sweet Valley wasn't established as a town until 1857."

"That is absolutely correct," Mrs. Arnette said with a smile. "Very good, Sandra."

Jessica frowned. What was happening to Sandra? It wasn't just her looks anymore. She had learned something from the twins' lessons in confidence and poise, too. Just one little make-over, and suddenly Sandra had come to life. Jessica felt like she'd created a monster, and now, she was the one getting left behind.

"And to celebrate Sweet Valley Days here at school," Mrs. Arnette was saying, "our mayor, Mr. Herbert Lodge, will attend an assembly next week to talk to the entire school." She sat on the edge of her desk. "One sixth-grade social studies student will win the honor of introducing Mayor Lodge at the assembly," she continued. "The student must be someone who is a good citizen, a good student, and a good public speaker. Tomorrow I will be asking you to nominate the students you think would be most worthy. Then the final decision will be made by the social studies teachers and your principal, Mr. Clark."

Jessica smiled. How she would love to be the one to introduce Mayor Lodge! She could buy a new dress, or maybe design one herself. Everyone would be impressed with how pretty and well-spoken she was. Even Mayor Lodge would compliment her.

"And don't forget, students," Mrs. Arnette was saying, "there is one other honor you might want to try for. As always, the highlight of Sweet Valley Days will be a parade through downtown Sweet Valley, led by the citizenship float. In past years, only high school students have ridden on that float. This year, one student from *each* grade will be chosen to ride."

"Will the social studies teachers pick that person, too?" Elizabeth asked.

"No, the sixth-grade Citizen of the Year will be

elected by all the sixth-grade students. But remember, this is not a popularity contest. The student who wins must be an outstanding citizen, dedicated to making Sweet Valley a better place to live."

Now Jessica was really excited. Riding on the citizenship float would be a real honor. Plus, the kids who won got to dress in pioneer clothes—old-fashioned suits and string ties for the boys and ankle-length dresses for the girls. What a thrill it would be to dress up like that and parade down the street with the whole town watching!

But Jessica had another reason for wanting to win. If she was selected to introduce the mayor *and* ride in the Sweet Valley Days parade, it would be the talk of the school. The thought made Jessica feel good. After all the attention Sandra Ferris had been getting, she felt she deserved a little for herself. And this was the perfect way to get it.

As soon as class ended, Jessica turned to her twin. "Elizabeth," she said, "I want you to nominate me to introduce the mayor."

"You do?" Elizabeth asked, surprised. "I thought you'd want to run for sixth-grade Citizen of the Year. I mean, wouldn't you rather ride in the parade than introduce the mayor?"

Jessica just smiled. "I don't have to choose one or the other. I'm going to do both."

Six

◇

When school ended that day, Elizabeth and Sandra headed for Elizabeth's house to bake cookies.

"I like your outfit," Elizabeth remarked as they walked down the street to her house.

Sandra was wearing a salmon-colored blouse and a denim miniskirt. "Do you really?" she asked uncertainly. "I mean, you're not just saying that to be nice, are you?"

"What do you mean?" Elizabeth asked. "Why would I?"

Sandra wasn't sure how to explain her feelings. She hardly understood them herself. "I don't know," she began. "It's just that everybody used to treat me like I was a real nerd. Then you and Jessica gave me that make-over, and all of a sudden, everything changed. It happened so quickly."

"But what's wrong with that?" Elizabeth asked as they let themselves into her house through the kitchen door.

Sandra shrugged helplessly. "Nothing's wrong with it—it's really fun. But I feel like I'm in a dream and one day soon I'm going to wake up and it'll all be over."

"Don't be silly. Everyone at school likes you. Why should that change?"

Before Sandra could answer, Steven appeared. "I thought I heard voices. Hi, Lizzie. Hi, Sandra." He moved closer and smiled at Sandra. "I'm still waiting to play volleyball with you. How about this Saturday?"

"I—I don't know," Sandra said shyly. She shrugged and looked away.

Steven looked disappointed. "Well, maybe I'll see you there." He turned and walked slowly out of the room.

Elizabeth waited until Steven was gone. Then she said, "I thought you loved volleyball. Why don't you want to go?"

"I do want to," Sandra said. "But Steven is older than I am, and lots more popular. Why would he want to do anything with me?"

"Because he likes you, silly. Can't you tell? It's written all over his face."

"But doesn't he care about the way I used to look? You know, before the make-over?"

"What's the difference?" Elizabeth asked, reaching up to get the flour from the cabinet. "You're still the same person."

"But what would happen if I stopped buying new clothes?" Sandra asked anxiously. "Or if I didn't have time to fix my hair one morning?" Suddenly, her eyes filled with tears. "Then everything would go back to the way it used to be. I'd just be stupid old Sandra the Nerd, and everyone would start laughing at me again."

"Sandra, don't be silly," Elizabeth said. "It's not just the way you look that makes people like you. Oh, sure, maybe it seems that way now. All the kids are so amazed to see your new look that they're paying a lot of attention to you. But you're a sweet, friendly person. That's why people like you."

Sandra wanted to believe it, but she still wasn't sure. "I don't know," she said, reaching up to wipe away the tears. "I feel so confused."

Elizabeth leaned against the counter and looked at her friend. "What would it take to make you believe that people really like you?"

Sandra thought it over. *What more will it take to make me believe in myself?* she wondered.

Then all at once she had an idea. What if she was the one chosen to introduce the mayor at the assembly next week? It wasn't good looks or fancy clothes that counted in a contest like that. It was good grades, and confidence, and the ability to speak in front of the whole school. If Sandra won, then she would know for sure that she was as smart and talented as the other girls at school. And everyone else would know it, too.

"Elizabeth," she said hesitantly, "I was wondering . . . that is, I thought . . ." She took a deep breath and blurted it out. "Would you nominate me to introduce the mayor in next week's assembly?"

Elizabeth hesitated. "Gee, I'd like to, but Jessica asked me to nominate her."

"Oh, please, Elizabeth. Please! Jessica gets picked for lots of things. But I've never won anything."

"Well . . ."

"It would mean so much to me!" Sandra cried.

"But what if you don't win?" Elizabeth asked.

"Just being nominated by you would be special," she answered. "Please, Elizabeth, will you do it?"

Elizabeth looked at Sandra in silence. Then she smiled and said, "Of course I will."

"Oh, thank you!" Sandra threw her arms around Elizabeth and gave her a big hug.

"You're welcome" Elizabeth laughed. "And now, would you do a favor for me?"

"Anything!"

"Help me make the cookies. I'm absolutely starving!"

Sandra laughed. With a grin, she grabbed the sugar and eggs. "On your mark," she exclaimed, "get set, start mixing!"

After dinner, Jessica went up to her room to get the drawing pad that contained all of her fashion designs. Until now, she hadn't shown her designs to anyone except Elizabeth and Sandra. But tonight she felt it was time to show them to someone who really knew about designing—her mother. Mrs. Wakefield worked part-time as an interior designer, and she knew a great deal about art and color and design. *If Mom likes my fashion ideas,* Jessica told herself, *it will mean I'm really good.*

Mrs. Wakefield was sitting at the dining room table, paying bills. "Mom," Jessica said as she walked into the room, "can I show you something?"

"Of course, dear," Mrs. Wakefield replied with a smile. "Sit down."

Jessica took a seat and handed her mother the drawing pad. Mrs. Wakefield opened it and leafed through the pages. Jessica fidgeted impatiently, nibbling on her fingernails as she waited.

"Why, Jessica," her mother said at last, "I had no idea that you were this interested in fashion design."

"Do you like them?" Jessica asked anxiously. "I mean, are they any good?"

"They're quite good," Mrs. Wakefield said. "I like them very much."

"Then do you think I could be a fashion designer when I grow up?"

Mrs. Wakefield closed the drawing pad and sat back in her chair. "You can certainly give it a try. It's not an easy profession, though. There's a great deal of competition."

"But you think my ideas are good, don't you?"

"Yes, of course. But that's not all it takes. You have to work hard and practice your drawing. And you have to be able to sew."

"I can sew," Jessica said. "I sewed those lace cuffs and collar onto my sweater."

"Yes, but you told me that one of them fell off, didn't you?" Mrs. Wakefield asked.

"That wasn't my fault!" Jessica insisted.

Mrs. Wakefield smiled. "Why don't I give you some sewing lessons?" she suggested. "We could start with something simple, like sewing a hem. Then you could work up to making an apron, or even a skirt."

"An apron! Mom, that's boring. Why can't I sew one of my fashion ideas?" Then suddenly Jessica had a wonderful idea. "Wait a minute!" she cried. "Next weekend is Sweet Valley Days, and I'm going to run for sixth-grade Citizen of the Year. If I win, I'll get to wear a pioneer dress and ride on the citizenship float."

Mrs. Wakefield looked puzzled. "But what does that have to do with sewing?" she asked.

"I'm going to design a dress to wear on the float. And then you can help me make it!"

"But, Jessica," Mrs. Wakefield warned, "a dress like that would be very difficult to make. Don't you think you should start with something simpler?"

But Jessica wasn't listening. She was imagining herself riding on the citizenship float in her beautiful pioneer dress. In her fantasy, everyone was waving to her and she was smiling down at them and waving back.

"Jessica?"

Mrs. Wakefield's voice brought Jessica back to the present. "I'm going upstairs to start designing my dress right now," she said. She hopped up from her chair and leaned over to kiss her mother on the cheek. "Thanks for all your help, Mom!" Before Mrs. Wakefield could answer, Jessica rushed out of the room and ran upstairs.

She was hard at work when Elizabeth knocked on her door a few minutes later. "Can I come in?" Elizabeth asked.

"OK, but make it fast. I'm designing a dress to wear in the Sweet Valley Days parade."

"So you're definitely going to run for sixth-grade Citizen of the Year?" Elizabeth asked.

Jessica turned from her artwork. "Of course. And I think I have a good chance of winning, too. Mrs. Arnette said it's not a popularity contest, but being popular sure can't hurt. And since I'm a Unicorn, everyone knows I'm pretty special."

"Does that mean you don't want me to nominate you to introduce the mayor?" Elizabeth asked hopefully.

"Of course I do. Don't you remember? I told you I want to win both."

"Oh." Elizabeth hesitated. "Jess," she said at last, "I told Sandra I'd nominate her."

Jessica could hardly believe her ears. "Sandra Ferris? But you promised *me*!"

"I know. But Sandra really needs something like this to build up her confidence."

"Are you kidding?" Jessica cried. "Have you seen her sitting at the Unicorn table? Or flirting with Bruce Patman? That girl's got all the confidence she needs!"

"Not really. She's definitely enjoying the attention, but deep down she's still shy and tongue-tied," Elizabeth explained. "In fact, when she asked me to nominate her, she was close to tears."

Jessica hardly knew what to say. Sandra already had a new look, new friends, and more attention than she'd ever had in her life. And now, as if that wasn't enough, Sandra wanted Elizabeth to nominate *her* instead of Jessica to introduce the mayor. It just wasn't fair.

Jessica threw down the colored pencil she was holding and got up from her desk. "If you ask me," she said unhappily, "Sandra is just pretending to be shy to get what she wants."

Elizabeth shook her head. "I don't believe that. Sandra is a nice person. Besides, what do you care if I nominate her to introduce the mayor? That's not as important as riding on the citizenship float in the parade."

"I know, but I wanted to win both," Jessica said with a pout. "And anyway, you promised to nominate me."

"But I'll still nominate you for sixth-grade Citizen of the Year," Elizabeth said. When Jessica didn't answer, Elizabeth walked over to her twin and looked her in the eye. "Be honest, Jess," she said. "You have a much better chance of winning Citizen of the Year. And it's the one you really want, isn't it?"

Jessica thought it over. She did want to ride on the float more than she wanted to introduce the mayor. Besides, she was sure Sandra wouldn't win that honor either. After all, Mrs. Arnette said that the person who introduced the mayor had to be a good public speaker, and Sandra never spoke in front of large groups of people. Why, until this week she hadn't even had the nerve to raise her hand in class!

"Oh, all right," Jessica said finally. "Go ahead and nominate Sandra."

Elizabeth threw her arms around her sister and hugged her. "Thanks, Jess!"

"But if you ask me, she's a schemer," Jessica said. "She wants all the attention for herself, and she'll do anything to get it."

"Oh, come on, Jessica," Elizabeth said. "Where did you get such a crazy idea?"

Jessica couldn't explain it. It was just something she felt inside. "Just wait and see," was all she said.

Seven

◇

In social studies the next day, Mrs. Arnette asked the class for nominations for the student who would introduce Mayor Lodge at the Sweet Valley Days assembly. Pamela Jacobson and Brooke Dennis nominated each other, and Jim Sturbridge nominated himself.

"Anyone else?" Mrs. Arnette asked, glancing around the room.

Elizabeth raised her hand. "I nominate Sandra Ferris."

Mrs. Arnette looked a bit surprised. Then she smiled and wrote down the name.

Jessica was sitting in the back of the room, trying to look as if she couldn't care less who her sister nominated. But inside she felt angry and jealous. She glanced over at Sandra. Sandra's cheeks were flushed and she looked excited and nervous.

Jessica looked away. She was beginning to wish she could take back the make-over she'd done on Sandra. She thought about what Caroline Pearce had told her. *Janet Howell wants Sandra to join the Unicorns.* So far, Janet hadn't mentioned it. But what if it *was* true?

To make herself feel better, Jessica opened her notebook and started sketching some ideas for her pioneer dress. The more she drew, the better she felt. She was certain she could win the election for sixth-grade Citizen of the Year without very much effort.

When school ended, Jessica hurried to the school office. Mrs. Arnette had promised she would post the name of the person selected to introduce the mayor, and Jessica wanted to be first to see it. As she walked down the hall, she felt a smile creep over her face. She was positive Sandra hadn't won. She could hardly wait to find Elizabeth and say, "I told you so."

But when she turned the corner to the office, she saw that Sandra and Elizabeth were already there. "I won!" Sandra was almost shouting. "I won!"

Jessica's smile disappeared. "Let me see that," she

muttered, pushing past Sandra to look at the piece of paper Mrs. Arnette had posted on the office door. Sure enough, Sandra had been selected to introduce the mayor.

"I can't believe it," Sandra said. "I've never won anything in my life. I just hope I can get up in front of the whole assembly without fainting!"

"You can do it," Elizabeth said. "All you have to do is believe in yourself."

"You know," Sandra said, "I think I finally *do* believe in myself." She gave Elizabeth a hug. "Thanks, Elizabeth. I owe it all to you."

Jessica glared at Sandra. How could Sandra say she owed everything to Elizabeth? The whole idea was ridiculous. *If it wasn't for that make-over I gave her,* Jessica thought furiously, *Sandra would still be a complete nerd.*

"I don't think I've ever been so happy in my whole life," Sandra was saying. "I feel like I could do absolutely anything." She laughed. "I feel like Wonder Woman."

Then suddenly, Sandra's eyes grew wide. "I just had the neatest idea. It's crazy, but . . . I think I might run for sixth-grade Citizen of the Year." She turned to Jessica. "What do you think, Jessica? Do I have a chance?"

Jessica was speechless. First Sandra had convinced Elizabeth to nominate her to introduce the mayor. Now she was after the Citizen of the Year award, too.

"I don't think Jessica's the person to ask," Elizabeth said softly. "She plans to run for Citizen of the Year herself."

"Oh. Sorry, Jessica," Sandra said. Then she added, "I probably don't have a chance against someone like you. But I think I'll run anyway. It sounds like fun." She ran off to share her good news.

"She's right about one thing," Jessica said flatly. "She doesn't have a chance."

"Jessica!" Elizabeth said.

"I don't care. It's just not fair. Sandra wants to win everything—even Citizen of the Year."

"So what?" Elizabeth said. "You wanted to win both honors, too."

Jessica knew Elizabeth was right. But she didn't care. She had already given up one honor to Sandra. She couldn't bear to give up another. "Let her run against me," she said huffily. "There's no way she'll win!" Then she turned and stomped off down the hall.

The next day was Saturday. That morning, Jessica met Janet Howell, Lila Fowler, and Kimberly Haver at the Valley Mall.

"Did you hear about Sandra Ferris?" Lila asked as

the girls stopped for sodas at Casey's Place. "She's going to introduce the mayor in the Sweet Valley Days assembly."

"That's not all," Jessica said irritably. "She's running for sixth-grade Citizen of the Year, too."

"That's a real honor," Kimberly said. "The kids who ride on the citizenship float will be famous all over Sweet Valley."

"I think one of the Unicorns should win," Janet said. "After all, we're the most special girls in the school."

Jessica took a deep breath. Then she said something she'd been wanting to say for days. "Janet," she began, "Caroline Pearce said you wanted Sandra to join the Unicorns."

The girls burst into giggles. "Are you kidding?" Janet laughed. "Sandra's nice, but she's not exactly Unicorn material."

Jessica let out a sigh of relief. She tossed her blond hair behind her shoulders and said casually, "You know, I was thinking of running for sixth-grade Citizen of the Year."

"Oh, Jess, you'd be perfect!" Kimberly exclaimed.

"And you're sure to beat Sandra," Janet agreed. "Everyone knows the Unicorns are the most popular girls in the school."

"Why don't you run for eighth-grade citizen, Janet?" Jessica suggested generously.

"And I'll run for seventh-grade," Kimberly said.

"Let's all work together to put three Unicorns on the citizenship float!" Janet exclaimed. All the girls agreed.

Jessica smiled. She felt better than she had in days. With all the Unicorns behind her, there was no way she could lose. But just to be on the safe side, she was going to make absolutely sure that every student in Sweet Valley Middle School knew she was a good citizen. Then they would be certain to vote for her instead of Sandra.

Jessica got her first chance to prove her citizenship in English class on Monday. Mr. Bowman took the class to the school library to learn how to use the *Reader's Guide to Periodical Literature*. As they walked in, Jessica noticed a metal can sitting on the desk of Ms. Luster, the school librarian. A sign on the can said, SWEET VALLEY LITERACY PROGRAM: GIVE GENEROUSLY SO THAT OTHERS MAY LEARN TO READ.

Jessica waited until the class was seated. Then she raised her hand. When Ms. Luster called on her, she said, "I noticed you're collecting money for the Sweet Valley Literacy Program. I hope everyone in the class will give some money." She walked to Ms. Luster's desk and picked up the can. "I'll start it off with one dollar."

Jessica was saving her allowance money to buy the new Johnny Buck album. Even so, she took a dollar from her purse and put it in the can.

"Why, Jessica, that's very generous of you," Ms. Luster said.

Suddenly, Sandra jumped to her feet. "Jessica's right," she announced. "It's important to support community programs. I'm donating two dollars." She walked to the front of the room and dropped two dollar bills in the can.

"Thank you *very* much, Sandra," Ms. Luster said. "Now let's get started with our lesson. Anyone else who would like to make a donation may do so at the end of class."

Jessica couldn't believe Sandra would pull such a dirty trick. *She doesn't give a hoot about the literacy program,* she thought angrily. *She just wants to show me up.* She shot Sandra a nasty look, but Sandra just ignored her.

The girls' next class together was social studies. Mrs. Arnette announced that Sandra had been selected to introduce the mayor. Then she reminded the class that the election for sixth-grade Citizen of the Year would be on Wednesday, and asked for nominations.

Olivia Davidson raised her hand. "I nominate Sandra Ferris," she said.

"My goodness," Mrs. Arnette exclaimed with surprise, "Sandra was nominated to introduce the mayor. Now she's being nominated again." She laughed. "Sandra, you certainly are popular."

Mrs. Arnette's words stung Jessica. Even teachers were paying more attention to Sandra these days.

Then Elizabeth raised her hand. "I nominate Jessica Wakefield," she said.

Mrs. Arnette nodded. "Anyone else?" she asked.

Jim Sturbridge nominated himself again, and Amy Sutton nominated Ken Matthews. Mrs. Arnette closed the nominations and picked up her lesson planner.

Jessica perked up a little. Jim was running as a joke, and although Ken was a nice guy, Jessica knew he wasn't popular enough to be a real threat. Now all Jessica had to do was figure out a way to convince the school she was a better citizen than Sandra.

Jessica spent the rest of the day trying. When social studies ended, Jessica offered to erase the blackboard. But while she was erasing it, Sandra went to Mrs. Arnette and offered to wash the board *and* clap the erasers. In gym class, Jessica missed an easy volleyball shot, but Sandra spiked the ball to win the game. In science, Jessica volunteered to clean out the gerbil cage, but Mr. Bailey told her that Sandra had already offered to do it.

By the time school ended, Jessica was furious. She caught up with Elizabeth outside by the bicycle rack.

"Can you believe what Sandra's doing?" she asked indignantly. "What a snake!"

"What do you mean?" Elizabeth asked. "What's she doing?"

"You know what I'm talking about. If I donate one dollar to the literacy program, she donates two. If I erase the blackboard, she offers to wash it. She's trying to show me up!"

Elizabeth smiled. "I think you're just mad because Sandra's beating you at your own game," she said.

"I am not!" Jessica cried. She turned to her twin. "Why are you sticking up for her? Don't you want your own sister to win the election?"

"Of course I do, Jess," Elizabeth said. "I just don't think you should criticize Sandra for doing exactly the same things you're doing. You both want to prove what good citizens you are. There's nothing wrong with that."

Jessica didn't answer. She was too busy thinking. Somehow she had to find a way to prove once and for all that she was a better citizen than Sandra. Everything she'd tried so far had backfired. *If only I could think of something really big,* she thought. *Something that even Sandra couldn't top.*

Then suddenly, she saw something that gave her an idea. A sign announcing a car wash sponsored by the Sweet Valley Public Library was taped to a telephone pole. According to the sign, the library needed money to repair their bookmobile. All month long they'd been sponsoring activities to raise money—a book sale, a bake sale, an auction. But they still didn't have enough.

If only I could think of a way for the middle school to raise the rest of that money, Jessica thought eagerly. *Everyone would be so impressed, they'd be sure to vote for me.* Somehow she was going to come up with the perfect plan to raise that money.

Eight

◇

All evening long, Jessica tried to think of different ways to raise money for the library bookmobile. It had to be something the whole school could be involved in. Something bigger and better than a bake sale or a car wash. But Jessica couldn't think of a thing.

After dinner, she went upstairs to work on her design for her pioneer dress. Over the weekend, she had checked out a book on the history of fashion from the public library. Using the illustrations in the book as a guide, she had filled almost an entire drawing pad with pictures.

Now her design was almost finished. She sat back in her chair and studied her picture. She had drawn a red-and-black plaid dress. It had a fitted waist and a full skirt that hung all the way to her ankles. The collar was high and lacy and there were buttons down the front.

Jessica chewed on the end of her pencil and furrowed her brow. There was something missing. But what? Then suddenly, she had an inspiration. Quickly, she drew a big black bow on the waist of the dress. Then she held up the pad and looked at her drawing. Perfect. Just perfect!

Jessica jumped up and ran downstairs to the family room. "Look, Mom," she cried, "I finished my design. This is the dress I want to wear in the Sweet Valley Days parade!" She held up the drawing pad for both her parents to see. "What do you think?"

"Why, that's beautiful, hon," Mr. Wakefield said. "You'll look like a real pioneer woman in that."

"It's lovely," Mrs. Wakefield agreed. "But it's not going to be easy to make. We'll have to go to the fabric store and see if we can find a pattern for a simple long dress. Then we'll try to modify it to create the dress you designed."

"We better go tomorrow after school," Jessica said. "The parade is this Saturday."

Mrs. Wakefield laughed and shook her head. "How do I get myself into these things?"

"Just be glad Elizabeth doesn't want to make one, too," Mr. Wakefield joked.

"All right, Jessica," Mrs. Wakefield said. "We'll go tomorrow after school. But be sure you don't make any other plans for the rest of the week. This dress is going to take every minute of your spare time."

Jessica couldn't believe it. How long could it take to make a pioneer dress? Not more than a few hours, surely. But to please her mother she said, "I promise."

Jessica turned to go back upstairs but then she remembered the bookmobile. Maybe her parents had an idea for raising the money. "Mom, Dad," she began, "if you wanted to raise a lot of money for a worthy cause, how would you do it?"

"A bake sale," Mrs. Wakefield suggested. "Or a car wash."

"It's got to be something bigger than that," Jessica said.

"Sweet Valley Hospital has a raffle every year," Mr. Wakefield mused. "They sell tickets and the winner takes home a new car."

"But if I had enough money to buy a car, I wouldn't need to raise the money in the first place," Jessica said.

"Good point. But the hospital asks one of the local car dealers to donate the car."

Jessica sighed. There was no way a local car dealer was going to donate a car to her. Besides, none of the kids at Sweet Valley Middle School would buy raffle tickets for a car—they weren't even old enough to drive. "Any other ideas?" Jessica asked hopefully.

"What do you need to raise money for?" Mr. Wakefield asked.

"The library. They need to repair their bookmobile. If I can think of a way to raise the money, I'll be sure to win the election for sixth-grade Citizen of the Year."

Mrs. Wakefield turned to face her daughter. "Jessica, you're getting awfully wrapped up in this election, aren't you? What if you don't win?"

Jessica didn't want to think about that. If she didn't win, she wouldn't be able to wear her pioneer dress in the parade. Besides, if she didn't win the election, someone else would—and that someone would almost certainly be Sandra Ferris.

"I'm not going to lose," she said firmly. "I'm going to win, no matter what!" She jumped up from the sofa and ran upstairs.

Later that night, Jessica lay in bed, tossing and turning. Her head was filled with worries and her stomach felt like one big knot. She rolled over and let out a long sigh. She had to win that election. She just *had* to. But to do that, she had to prove she was a better citizen than Sandra. *But how can I?* Jessica wondered unhappily. *I can't even think of a way to raise money for the library's bookmobile.*

Finally, Jessica gave up trying to go to sleep. She

got out of bed and wandered downstairs. Maybe if she drank a cup of herbal tea it would soothe her stomach.

The living room was dark, but there was a light on in the kitchen. Steven was standing at the counter, wolfing down a piece of cold chicken.

"Hi, Little Sis," he said. "Hope you didn't come down looking for the apple cake Mom made for dessert. I just ate the last piece."

Normally, Jessica would have been angry with Steven for eating so much, but tonight she didn't care. "All I want is a cup of tea," she said wearily.

"Hey, what's the matter with you?" Steven asked. "You look terrible."

Jessica usually didn't confide in Steven, but she was willing to try anything to win that election. "I need to think of a way to raise money to help the library repair their bookmobile. It's got to be something the whole middle school can do. Got any ideas?"

Steven chewed his chicken thoughtfully. "Well, last year when the seniors wanted to raise money for the prom, they published a commemorative booklet."

"What's that?" Jessica asked.

"A book about the prom, with lots of photos and stuff. Everyone who goes to the prom gets one."

"But how does that raise money?"

"Simple. The seniors went to all the local businesses and store owners and convinced them to put ads in the booklet. The money they made from selling the ads helped pay for the prom."

As Steven spoke, Jessica's eyes got bigger and bigger. What a fabulous idea! All she had to do was convince the middle school to put out a commemorative booklet about Sweet Valley Days. Then the students could sell ads to local stores and donate the profits to the library to repair their bookmobile.

"Steven, you're a genius!" she exclaimed. She leaned over and gave her brother a kiss on the cheek.

"Yech!" he cried. "Just because I'm brilliant doesn't mean you have to give me a disease."

Jessica just laughed. She could hardly wait to get to school to tell Mrs. Arnette about her idea. When the kids found out about her plan for the commemorative booklet, she was sure to win the election.

The next morning, Sandra left for school early. She was meeting Elizabeth at the school fountain so they could go over their math homework together.

As she pedaled her bike down the street, Sandra looked at her reflection in the side mirror. She was wearing her hair in a ponytail with a pink velvet bow. She had a touch of blusher on her cheeks and a light coating of lip gloss on her mouth, just the way Jessica and Elizabeth had showed her.

Sandra pedaled her bike into the school parking lot and parked it in the bike rack. She walked around the side of the school and headed for the fountain. She saw Elizabeth sitting on the edge of the fountain with Jessica.

Sandra stopped. She didn't want to talk to Jessica. She knew Jessica didn't really like her by the way she looked at her and talked to her.

Sandra couldn't understand it. She had always been nice to Jessica. After the make-over, she had even thought they were getting to be friends. But now Jessica seemed to dislike her more than ever. With every good thing that happened to Sandra, Jessica acted colder and colder. In fact, over the last few days, Jessica had barely said two words to her!

It's not right, Sandra thought. After all, Jessica had been popular ever since her first day at Sweet Valley Middle School. For Sandra, however, being popular was a new experience. It was her turn to shine and nothing was going to stop her. *I deserve to win the election*, she thought. *It's only fair. Jessica ought to understand*.

Sandra decided to wait until Jessica left. She moved closer to the fountain and stepped behind an oak tree. Now she could see the twins, but they couldn't see her. In fact, she could almost hear their conversation.

". . . the library needs money to repair their bookmobile," she heard Jessica say.

Sandra wondered what the twins were talking about. She knew the library was organizing car washes and book sales to raise money for the bookmobile. In fact, she planned to donate some money herself. Without realizing it, Sandra moved a little closer so she could hear better.

". . . and sell ads to raise the money," Jessica was saying.

Sell ads. Suddenly, Sandra remembered something her older sister, Heather, had told her. To raise money for last year's prom, the seniors at the high school had put out a booklet filled with pictures of the prom. Heather had written an article for the booklet about good places to eat breakfast after the prom. And the seniors had financed the booklet by selling ads to local stores.

All at once, Sandra had the most incredible idea. What if the middle school put out a commemorative booklet for Sweet Valley Days? All the kids could sell ads to local merchants. And the profit would be donated to fixing the library bookmobile!

Sandra was so excited she could hardly stand still. She was sure that when the kids heard about her plan, they'd all want to vote for her. And then she would get to ride on the citizenship float in the Sweet Valley Days parade!

Sandra could hardly wait to tell Mrs. Arnette about her idea. In fact, she was so impatient, she completely forgot about her meeting with Elizabeth. Instead, she hurried across the lawn to the school entrance. Someone was calling her name, but she didn't even turn around. There was no time to stop now. She had to talk to Mrs. Arnette right away.

Nine
◇

Jessica and Elizabeth looked up and saw Sandra running across the school lawn. "Hey, isn't that Sandra?" Jessica asked.

"Yes, it is," Elizabeth replied. She stood up and called to her friend. "Sandra! Sandra!" But Sandra ignored her and ran into the school.

"That's weird," Jessica said. "I thought she was supposed to meet you here before school started."

"She was. I don't know why she didn't stop."

Jessica stood up and collected her books. "Well, I'm going to talk to Mrs. Arnette now." She smiled. "I can't wait to tell her my idea for the Sweet Valley Days booklet."

"I guess I'll stay here a little longer in case Sandra comes back," Elizabeth said. "See you in homeroom."

Jessica hurried into the school. She was so excited, she practically ran down the hall. But when she reached Mrs. Arnette's classroom, the door was closed. She stood on tiptoe and peeked through the window. Sandra was inside, talking excitedly to Mrs. Arnette.

What could they be talking about? Jessica wondered. Just then, Mrs. Arnette stood up from her desk and walked with Sandra to the door. Jessica jumped aside just as the door opened. "Why, Jessica," Mrs. Arnette said when she saw her. "I didn't know you were out here."

"Yes, I was waiting to talk to you," Jessica explained.

"Well, I just finished with Sandra, so you can come right in." As Sandra stepped into the hallway, Mrs. Arnette added, "Sandra has a wonderful idea for a way to raise money for the public library. Their bookmobile needs repairs, you know."

"What?" Jessica gasped in alarm. "What idea?"

"I think the middle school should publish a commemorative booklet about Sweet Valley Days," Sandra explained. "The students can sell ads to local stores and the money they make will be donated to the bookmobile."

Jessica couldn't believe her ears. Sandra had stolen her idea! Jessica glared at her. But Sandra didn't even seem to notice.

"Well, come inside, Jessica," Mrs. Arnette said. She led Jessica into the room and closed the door. "What was it you wanted to talk to me about?"

Jessica didn't know what to say. She wanted to explain that the idea for the Sweet Valley booklet was hers. She wanted to tell Mrs. Arnette that Sandra had stolen her idea. But what proof did she have? "I . . . I . . . I just wanted to ask you what our homework assignment was for today," she said at last.

Mrs. Arnette peered over her glasses, fixing Jessica with a hard stare. "Weren't you listening when I gave it out in class yesterday?"

"Well, I . . . I guess I just forgot," Jessica lied.

"Hmm. You'll never be elected sixth-grade Citizen of the Year at this rate, young lady." She gave Jessica the assignment and added, "Sandra's idea about the Sweet Valley Days booklet is a fine one. If you truly want to be elected, you should try to develop as much community spirit as she has."

Jessica felt awful. It wasn't fair! Mrs. Arnette was praising Sandra for an idea that didn't even belong to her. Jessica felt tears welling up in her eyes. Quickly, she grabbed her books and hurried out into the hall. She lowered her head so no one would see her tears and walked quickly toward the girls' room.

Just as she reached the door, she saw Elizabeth coming around the corner. "Oh, Lizzie," Jessica called, "come quick. Something awful has happened."

Elizabeth ran down the hall to join her twin. They walked together into the empty girls' room. "What's wrong?" she asked with concern.

"Sandra stole my idea," Jessica said through hot tears.

"Stole it?" Elizabeth repeated. "What do you mean?"

"When I went to talk to Mrs. Arnette, Sandra was already there. And then Mrs. Arnette said that Sandra had thought up a wonderful idea to raise money to repair the library bookmobile." A tear trickled down Jessica's cheek and she reached up to wipe it away. "It was *my* idea, Lizzie—practically word for word!"

Elizabeth frowned. "But how could she steal it from you? You only told it to me ten minutes ago."

"Remember how we saw Sandra run past us out by the fountain?" Jessica asked. "Well, she must have been listening to us. When she heard my idea about the Sweet Valley Days booklet, she ran off to tell Mrs. Arnette before I could."

Elizabeth's mouth fell open. "But why would Sandra do something like that? It's not like her."

"That's what you think!" Jessica said indignantly. "I told you she was a schemer, didn't I? This just proves it."

"Well, maybe," Elizabeth admitted. "But we have to give Sandra a chance to explain herself. Let's go find her and talk to her about what happened."

Jessica took out a tissue and blew her nose. "All right," she said. "Let's go find her. Then you'll see I was right all along."

The twins walked through the school, looking for Sandra. They found her at her locker, hanging up her jacket. "Sandra, we need to talk to you," Elizabeth said.

Sandra closed her locker. "Sure. What about?"

"You stole my idea for the Sweet Valley Days booklet," Jessica said accusingly. "Admit it."

Sandra looked confused. "*Your* idea? What are you talking about?"

"Jessica told me her idea for the booklet this morning while we were sitting by the fountain," Elizabeth said.

"You were eavesdropping on us," Jessica said angrily. "You heard everything I said. And then you ran to tell Mrs. Arnette before I did."

"I wasn't eavesdropping," Sandra said. "I was just waiting for Jessica to leave."

"Then why did you run right past us?" Elizabeth

asked. "I called your name, but you didn't even turn around."

"I'm sorry, Elizabeth. I guess I was in a hurry to talk to Mrs. Arnette."

"About *my* idea!" Jessica cried.

Sandra looked upset. "Jessica," she said, "why are you being so mean to me? I don't want to fight with you. I want to be your friend."

"Friend?" Jessica said in astonishment. "I tried to be your friend. I gave you a make-over and lent you my clothes and everything. But you took all the credit yourself. And now you're doing it again!"

"What are you talking about?" Sandra said. "I never tried to take credit for anything that wasn't mine. I think you're just jealous because I might win the election."

"You don't deserve to win," Jessica cried. "You stole my idea, and that's cheating!"

Just then the bell rang for homeroom.

Sandra folded her arms across her chest and stared at Jessica. Tears were forming in the corners of her eyes. "You think you're something special, don't you, Jessica Wakefield?" She wiped her eyes with the back of her hand. "I never expected to win this election," she said, sniffling. "I just ran for the fun of it. But now I *want* to beat you, Jessica. And I'm going to do it, too. Just wait and see." With that, she turned and ran off down the hall.

Jessica watched Sandra go, too shocked to speak. Finally, she leaned against the lockers and let out a sigh. "I don't have a chance of winning the election now," she said miserably.

Elizabeth shook her head. "I think this is all a big misunderstanding. You just have to explain to Mrs. Arnette what happened. She'll know what to do."

"But I don't have any proof," Jessica said. "Besides, Sandra is one of Mrs. Arnette's favorite students. Why would the Hairnet believe me instead of her?"

"Well, then, we'll tell all the sixth graders."

"Forget it," Jessica said glumly. "Ever since we gave Sandra that make-over, she's been the talk of the school. If I say she stole my idea, the kids will think I'm just jealous."

"Maybe you're right," Elizabeth admitted. "But it just doesn't seem fair. There must be some way you and Sandra can work things out."

Jessica shrugged her shoulders. "Forget it, Lizzie. Come on, we'd better get going. We're going to be late for homeroom."

That afternoon, the entire school filed into the auditorium for the Sweet Valley Days assembly. Sandra stood at the side of the stage, waiting nervously for the moment when she would introduce Mayor Lodge. Her knees were shaking and her stomach was full of butterflies. She peeked around the corner of the curtain to find a full house.

Sandra took a deep breath and tried to remember her speech. What if her mind went blank when she started talking? *I'll just die of embarrassment*, she thought anxiously.

Mrs. Arnette was standing in the wings, talking with the mayor. She walked over to Sandra. "I have some good news, Sandra," she said. "I spoke to Mr. Clark about your idea for the Sweet Valley Days booklet. He was very impressed, just as I was. We both think it would be a wonderful project for the middle school."

"Wow!" Sandra exclaimed. "That's great!"

Mrs. Arnette smiled. "That's not all. We want you to announce your idea to the school right now."

"Now?" Sandra asked. "But I have to introduce the mayor."

"I'm sure he'll be just as interested to hear your idea as I was. Besides, you deserve to be the one who announces it to the school."

Sandra was so thrilled, she could hardly think straight. The principal had approved her idea! And now she was going to talk about it in front of the entire school.

But deep down, Sandra felt a little uneasy. She thought back to her conversation with Jessica and Elizabeth at her locker that morning. She could still hear Jessica's angry words: *You took all the credit yourself. And now you're doing it again.* The memory of it made Sandra feel like crying.

Why is Jessica so mad at me? she wondered. She hadn't been eavesdropping. Maybe she had heard a few words of Jessica and Elizabeth's conversation, but that was all. And anyway, she hadn't stolen Jessica's idea. She was certain of that.

Just then the curtain began to rise. That was Sandra's cue. Her heart started pounding and her legs felt weak. She took a deep breath, crossed her fingers, and walked out onto the stage.

"Good a-afternoon, everyone," she stammered. She winced. She was sure everyone was going to laugh at her. But no one did. With a sigh of relief, she cleared her throat and continued. "Before I introduce our guest, Mayor Lodge, I'd like to tell you about an idea I had to raise money for the public library's bookmobile."

Sandra explained her idea to the school. As she spoke, she felt more and more confident. "I hope all of you will do your best to sell lots of ads for the Sweet Valley Days booklet," she said. "The men and women who founded Sweet Valley were good citizens. They cared about this town and they worked hard to make it a good place to live. Now it's our turn. Let's follow in their footsteps and do our part to help Sweet Valley. Thank you."

Everyone applauded. Even the mayor was clapping. "And now," Sandra said, "I'd like to introduce a man who has dedicated his life to helping our community. Our mayor, Mr. Herbert Lodge."

Sandra walked off the stage. As she passed the mayor, he stopped to shake her hand. "That was a good introduction," he said. "I wish you a lot of luck with your Sweet Valley Days booklet."

Sandra felt like she was walking on air. Everyone liked her idea—even the mayor! Suddenly, her unpleasant conversation with Jessica and Elizabeth didn't seem so important. All that really mattered was winning the election and becoming sixth-grade Citizen of the Year. Sandra smiled. *The way things are going,* she thought happily, *there's no way I can lose!*

Ten

◇

That afternoon, Jessica and Elizabeth walked home from school together. They let themselves in through the kitchen door and tossed their books on the counter. A moment later, Steven came bounding down the stairs. When he saw the twins, his face registered disappointment.

"Oh, it's just you two," he said.

"Who were you expecting," Jessica said. "The president of the United States?"

"Naw. I thought Sandra might be with you," he said.

"You might as well forget about Sandra," Elizabeth

said sadly. "She won't be coming home with us anymore."

Steven looked disappointed. "Why not? Did you two have a fight or something?"

"Worse," Jessica said. She told her brother all about how Sandra had stolen her idea for the Sweet Valley Days booklet.

Steven looked as if someone had just slapped him across the face. "But—but Sandra seemed so nice."

Just then, Mrs. Wakefield walked into the kitchen with her purse over her shoulder. "Hello, girls. Well, Jessica, are you ready to go?"

"Go where?"

"Have you forgotten?" Mrs. Wakefield asked. "I promised to take you to the fabric store this afternoon to buy a pattern for your pioneer dress."

"Oh, that." Jessica let out a sigh. "I don't have any reason to make that dumb old dress now. There's no way I'm going to win the election."

"But why not, honey? Last night you were so sure you would win."

Quickly, Jessica explained how Sandra had stolen her idea.

"Calling someone a thief is a very serious claim," Mrs. Wakefield said. "Are you absolutely sure she didn't come up with the idea herself, Jessica?"

"How could she have? It was my idea exactly. Besides, we saw Sandra run into the school right after I told Elizabeth about it. She didn't even stop when we called her name."

Elizabeth shook her head. "I keep thinking it must be some kind of misunderstanding. I just can't believe Sandra would do something like that."

"She was eavesdropping," Jessica insisted. "I'm sure of it."

Mrs. Wakefield sighed. "Well, it certainly sounds as if Sandra acted unfairly." She walked over to Jessica and gave her a hug. "Poor Jessica. I know how unhappy you must feel. But I'm sure you can think up another idea to help you win the election."

"It's too late," Jessica said. "The election is tomorrow morning."

"Oh, dear," Mrs. Wakefield said sympathetically. "Well, try not to take it too hard, honey. There will be other honors to win. And even if you don't get to ride in the parade, it'll still be fun to make that pioneer dress."

"But you said it was going to be a lot of hard work," Jessica complained.

Mrs. Wakefield nodded. "It will be. But that doesn't mean it won't be fun. And remember, if you're going to be a fashion designer someday, you need to know how to put a dress together."

"Yeah, I guess so," Jessica said reluctantly.

Mrs. Wakefield leaned against the counter and looked at her children. "It seems like all three of you could use some cheering up." She smiled. "Come on, let's go to the fabric store together. Afterwards, we can stop at Casey's Place for some ice cream."

"All right!" Steven shouted. "I never say no to ice cream."

"That sounds great, Mom," Elizabeth agreed.

Jessica managed a half-hearted smile. The promise of an ice cream cone wasn't enough to make her forget her troubles. But she felt a little better. "OK," she said, turning her half-smile into a real one, "let's go."

The next day was election day. At the end of social studies class, Mrs. Arnette led her students to the auditorium to cast their votes for sixth-grade Citizen of the Year.

Sandra stood in line waiting for her turn to vote. She was so nervous she could hardly breathe. She wanted to win the election more than anything in the world. She closed her eyes and pictured herself riding on the citizenship float. The thought made her feel good all over.

The first person to come out of the voting booth was Olivia Davidson. As she passed Sandra she whispered, "I voted for you!"

Sandra grinned. "Thanks!" she whispered back.

Brooke Dennis went next. As she passed Sandra, she gave her the thumbs-up sign. Next came Jim

Sturbridge. "You're going to win by a landslide," he said under his breath. "I didn't even vote for myself!"

The next person to walk into the voting booth was Jessica. As Sandra watched her, she thought about the fight she had had with Jessica and Elizabeth the morning before. No matter how hard she tried, she couldn't stop worrying about it. Sandra knew she hadn't stolen Jessica's idea. But then why did she have such an uneasy feeling in the pit of her stomach?

Jessica walked out of the voting booth. The hard, unsmiling look on her face stung Sandra. She felt tears welling up in her eyes, but she held them back.

Elizabeth was the next person to vote. Sandra couldn't pretend she didn't care what Elizabeth thought of her. *She was nice to me when everyone else thought I was a nerd*, Sandra thought.

But what about now? Yesterday, Elizabeth had seemed almost as mad as Jessica. But Sandra couldn't believe her friend was still angry with her. *It was just a misunderstanding*, she told herself. *That's all*.

When Elizabeth walked past, Sandra caught her eye and smiled. Elizabeth didn't smile back. She just gazed at Sandra with a disappointed look in her eyes.

Sandra felt awful. Why were Jessica and Elizabeth being so nasty? She was still wondering about it when Pamela Jacobson came out of the voting booth. As she walked by Sandra, she whispered, "Everyone's voting for you!"

Sandra smiled. What did it matter if Jessica and Elizabeth didn't like her? Everyone else did, and they were all voting for her. Finally, it was Sandra's turn to vote. She stepped into the voting booth, picked up a pencil, and checked off her name on the ballot.

When school ended that afternoon, Sandra grabbed her books and hurried to her locker. As she walked past the school office, Mrs. Arnette stepped into the hall. "Sandra," she said, "come in here a moment, please."

Sandra followed Mrs. Arnette into the office. "What is it?" she asked.

"This is supposed to be a secret until tomorrow, but I thought you'd like to know. We just counted the ballots and you won. You're sixth-grade Citizen of the Year! Congratulations!"

"Oh, wow!" Sandra cried. She was so happy she felt like throwing her arms around Mrs. Arnette and kissing her. "I won again! I can't believe it!"

"Jessica Wakefield is the runner-up. She'll be taking your place if you can't do it for some reason." Mrs. Arnette smiled. "Now, run along. The results will be made public tomorrow morning and then you can celebrate with your friends."

Sandra practically skipped down the hall. But by the time she reached the front of the school, her happiness had faded a little. Deep down she knew she couldn't feel truly happy about winning the election until she made up with the twins.

As she walked across the grassy lawn, Sandra made a decision. *I'm going to Jessica and Elizabeth's house to talk to them right now,* she told herself. Somehow she had to convince them she wasn't a cheater. Sandra wasn't sure if the twins would listen. All she knew was that she had to try.

Sandra hurried to the Wakefields' house. Steven was in the driveway, dribbling the basketball. When Sandra saw him, her heart beat wildly. She remembered what Elizabeth had told her the week before. *He likes you. It's written all over his face.*

Sandra liked Steven, too, even if she still felt too shy to do anything about it. She patted her hair in place and smiled. "Hi, Steven," she said.

Steven looked up. "Oh, it's you," he said with a frown.

The look on Steven's face made Sandra feel awful. "I—I came over to talk to Jessica and Elizabeth," she said uneasily.

"Well, I don't think they want to talk to you. Not after what you did to Jessica."

"But I *didn't* do anything," Sandra cried. "Honest I didn't."

"You didn't?" Steven said hopefully.

"No, of course not." She sighed. "I just wish I had some way to prove it."

Steven thought it over. "Tell me this," he said. "When did you think up the idea for the Sweet Valley Days booklet?"

"Yesterday morning," Sandra answered. "Right before school started."

Steven frowned. "Jessica thought of the idea the night before that. She asked me if I knew a good way to raise money. I told her about the commemorative booklet the high school puts out to make money for the prom. Then she decided to talk to her teacher about publishing a Sweet Valley Days booklet."

Sandra felt confused. "The night before? Are you sure?"

"Of course I'm sure." Steven looked at her sadly. "I don't get it, Sandra." He shook his head. "I just don't understand why you'd do something like this."

"But, Steven—" Sandra began.

"See you around." He picked up his basketball and went inside the house.

Sandra just stood in the driveway, watching him go. She felt stunned and sick. *Could Steven be right?* she wondered.

Sandra tried to think back on everything that had happened yesterday morning. She remembered standing behind the oak tree, waiting for Jessica to leave. She hadn't meant to listen to what the twins were saying, but she remembered hearing a few words. What were they? Something about the bookmobile. She closed her eyes and tried to think. Suddenly, Jessica's words came back to her: *". . . and sell ads to raise the money."*

Sandra gasped. Maybe she *had* overheard Jessica telling Elizabeth about the Sweet Valley Days booklet! Or at least she'd heard enough to figure the rest out for herself.

Then that means I really am a cheater, she told herself. The thought made her feel sick inside.

Sandra turned and walked slowly down the driveway. Since last Friday she had dreamed about winning the election for sixth-grade Citizen of the Year. Now that she had won it she felt troubled and confused. She let out a long, weary sigh. *What do I do now?* she wondered.

Eleven

◇

Saturday dawned bright and sunny, with hardly a cloud in the sky. But the way Jessica and Elizabeth were feeling, it might as well have been snowing. It was the morning of the Sweet Valley Days Parade.

Mrs. Wakefield made waffles for breakfast, but Jessica was too unhappy to eat. She pushed a piece of waffle around her plate with her fork and sighed. "Sandra must be getting ready for the parade now."

"I suppose so," Elizabeth agreed. "It starts in a couple of hours."

"I'll bet she's styling her hair in a French braid, just the way I taught her," Jessica said bitterly.

"And putting on lip gloss and blusher like we did for her make-over," Elizabeth added.

Mrs. Wakefield took a sip of her coffee. "At least you have the satisfaction of knowing you were the runner-up, Jessica," she pointed out.

Jessica shrugged. "A lot of good it does me."

"It would if Sandra got sick or something," Elizabeth said. "Then you'd have to take her place."

"In that case, I hope she comes down with pneumonia," Steven said meanly.

"All right, you three, that's enough," Mr. Wakefield interrupted. "I know you're unhappy, but there's no need to be unkind."

"But I can't help it," Jessica said with a pout. "If it weren't for Sandra Ferris, I would be the one getting ready to ride on the citizenship float."

"And wearing your pioneer dress, too," Elizabeth added.

Jessica had been working so hard on her pioneer dress. With her mother's help, she had finished everything except the hem. Designing and sewing her very own dress had been fun. But knowing that she wouldn't be wearing the dress in the parade had taken away a lot of the excitement.

"Have you finished hemming it yet?" Mrs. Wakefield asked.

"Why bother?" Jessica replied. "I don't have anywhere to wear it."

"You could wear it to the parade," Mr. Wakefield suggested. "Even if you aren't riding on the float, it would still look nice."

"Well, maybe," Jessica said, but her heart wasn't in it. "May I be excused?" she asked, pushing her plate of half-eaten waffles aside.

"Me, too," Elizabeth said.

"All right, girls," Mr. Wakefield replied. "Now, don't forget, we'll be leaving for the parade at ten-thirty. And I want to see both of you down here with smiles on your faces. OK?"

"We'll try, Daddy," Elizabeth said. She followed her twin out of the dining room. "What are you going to do until we leave?" she asked.

Jessica shrugged. "Hem my dress, I guess. How about you?"

"I'm going out to the thinking seat," she answered. The thinking seat was a low branch of the big pine tree in the backyard. Elizabeth went there whenever she wanted to do some serious thinking. "I'm still trying to figure out how Sandra and you could both have had the same idea for the Sweet Valley Days booklet," she explained.

"Easy," Jessica replied. "Sandra stole my idea. I told you that from the beginning."

"But, Jess—"

"Don't tell me you're still sticking up for her!"

Elizabeth shook her head. "No, not really. But

Sandra and I were getting to be good friends. I thought I knew her. There's just got to be some logical explanation."

Jessica smiled at her twin. "You always believe the best about people," she said fondly. "But no matter how long you sit and think, you can't change what Sandra did."

Elizabeth let out a long sigh. "Maybe you're right," she answered.

Elizabeth went outside and Jessica trudged upstairs to her room. She opened the closet door and stared at the pioneer dress hanging on her closet door.

The dress was far from perfect. The right sleeve was about an inch longer than the left one. The row of buttons that ran down the bodice was crooked. The waist was bunched up on the sides. In fact, the only part of the dress that looked right was the zipper, and that was because Mrs. Wakefield had put it in herself.

Who cares? Jessica thought glumly. *I won't be wearing the dress on the citizenship float, so what does it matter if it looks good or not?*

She pulled the dress off the hanger and took out her mother's sewing box. She turned on the radio to her favorite rock station, sat down on the bed, and started stitching the hem. Soon she was lost in the music and barely noticed what she was sewing.

Several minutes later, the sound of the doorbell startled her. Tossing aside the dress, she ran downstairs and opened the door. When she saw who it was, she let out a gasp. Sandra Ferris was standing there, dressed in shorts and a T-shirt!

"Hi, Jessica," she said shyly.

"What are you doing here?" Jessica asked curtly.

"I . . . I need to talk to you."

"Why aren't you dressed for the parade?"

"I've decided I'm not going to be in the parade," Sandra answered.

"What? Why not?"

Sandra shuffled nervously. "Can I come in?" she asked. "It's important."

Just then, Elizabeth walked in from the kitchen. When she saw Sandra, she rushed over to join her twin. "What's going on?" she asked.

"Oh, Elizabeth," Sandra said sadly, "I feel so awful."

"Come in," Elizabeth said. "Tell us what's wrong."

Sandra walked into the living room. "I want to apologize," she said, looking down at the floor. "You . . . were right, Jessica. I did steal your idea."

"I knew it!" Jessica cried.

"But I didn't mean to," she added quickly. "Honest, I didn't. Remember that morning I was supposed to meet Elizabeth at the fountain? I was standing behind the oak tree waiting for you to leave, Jessica. While I was there, I accidentally over-heard what you were saying. Not all of it—just the part about selling ads to raise money for the book-mobile."

"I told you so!" Jessica said to her sister.

"Quiet, Jess," Elizabeth said. "Let her talk."

"What you said reminded me of something my big sister had told me," Sandra continued. "Her class raised money for their prom by publishing a com-memorative booklet and selling ads to local busi-nesses." She looked at Jessica. "That's when I got the idea for a Sweet Valley Days booklet. I was so excited about it, I didn't even realize I'd overheard you talk-ing about the same thing."

"So you didn't really steal the idea after all," Eliza-beth said. "Not on purpose, anyway."

"But that's no excuse," Sandra said firmly. "Jessica had the idea first. I should have believed her when she told me that."

"Well, why didn't you?" Jessica asked.

Sandra shrugged helplessly. "I don't know. Ever since you gave me the make-over, everything's been happening so fast. One day I was a nobody, the next day I was the center of attention. I guess it just went to my head."

Elizabeth nodded sympathetically. "I remember what you told me the day we made cookies together. You were afraid people were only interested in you because of your new look. You weren't sure they liked you for who you really are."

"I guess deep down I didn't feel I deserved all the attention," Sandra explained. "That's why I wanted to win the contest to introduce the mayor—to prove to myself I was special. But I still wasn't convinced. So I ran for sixth-grade Citizen of the Year."

"And you won that, too," Jessica pointed out.

"Yes," Sandra said. "But not fairly. That's why I'm here." She took a deep breath and said, "I've decided I don't deserve to ride on the citizenship float."

"But, Sandra—" Elizabeth began.

"I've made up my mind," Sandra said. "I called the parade chairman before I came over here and told him I'm too sick to ride in the parade. I said the runner-up would have to take my place." She turned to Jessica. "That's you."

Jessica was stunned. "You mean, you gave up your place on the float for me?"

Sandra nodded. "You deserve it."

Jessica could hardly believe her ears. She was so happy she felt like dancing across the living room. "Wow!" she exclaimed. "Thanks, Sandra. Thanks a lot."

Sandra smiled shyly. "You're welcome. To tell you the truth, I was pretty nervous about riding in the parade, anyway." She giggled. "I guess I'm just not cut out to be a celebrity."

"Maybe not," Elizabeth said, "but who cares? You don't have to win awards to make people like you."

Sandra smiled shyly, but before she could respond Mr. and Mrs. Wakefield and Steven walked downstairs. They were ready to leave for the parade. When Steven saw Sandra, he stopped in his tracks. "Hey, what's going on?" he asked.

Quickly, Elizabeth explained what had happened.

"Why, that's very kind of you, Sandra," Mrs. Wakefield said with a smile.

"Yeah," Steven agreed, giving Sandra a friendly punch on the arm. "Way to go, Sandra."

Sandra grinned happily. Then she said, "Jessica, I want you to know that when we go to school on Monday, I'm going to tell Mrs. Arnette that you had the idea for the Sweet Valley Days booklet first."

Jessica felt like hugging Sandra. Just minutes ago, she had felt absolutely miserable. Now suddenly, everything had turned around. Thanks to Sandra, Jessica was going to be allowed to ride on the parade float *and* take credit for her idea. She smiled with satisfaction. *After all, I'm only getting what I deserve,* she thought.

But then, Jessica's conscience began to bother her. Even though she had thought up the idea for the Sweet Valley Days booklet, she wasn't sure it was fair to take all the credit. After all, ever since the day Sandra told Mrs. Arnette about the idea, she had been working nonstop on the booklet. Jessica, on the other hand, had been much too mad at Sandra to do anything to help. She hadn't even sold a single ad!

"Sandra," Jessica said, "I want you to take credit for the Sweet Valley Days booklet. I might have thought up the idea first, but you did all the work."

"Are you sure?" Sandra asked, surprised.

"Yes. It's only fair. I'll ride in the parade and you'll take credit for the booklet. Is it a deal?"

Sandra was grinning from ear to ear. "Deal!" she said happily. "Thanks!"

"Well, kids," Mr. Wakefield broke in, "we'd better get going. Sandra, would you like to ride over to the parade with us."

"Yeah, Sandra," Steven said. "Come with us."

"Thanks," Sandra said with a shy smile.

Mrs. Wakefield put her arm around Jessica. "Now aren't you glad you made that pioneer dress?" she asked.

Jessica let out a gasp. "My pioneer dress! Oh, no! I didn't finish the hem. I can't wear it in the parade without a hem!"

"There's no time to finish it now," Mrs. Wakefield said. "We'll have to put up the hem with tape. Now, hurry and get dressed. The parade starts in half an hour."

Jessica flew up the stairs two at a time. Quickly, she slipped into her pioneer dress and pulled up the zipper. She looked in the mirror at the crooked row of buttons and the bunched-up waist. *If only I'd taken the time to make it perfect,* she thought with regret.

But there wasn't time to worry about that now. She had to hurry if she was going to make the parade on time. Quickly, Jessica grabbed a roll of tape and ran downstairs to join her family.

Twelve

◇

Everyone climbed into the van and Mr. Wakefield drove downtown. Jessica spent the whole ride taping up her hem. It was difficult to do in the moving car, and she couldn't be certain the hem was straight. Still, it was better than nothing.

Mr. Wakefield turned onto Blossom Boulevard. Jessica pressed her nose against the window and gasped with excitement. The entire boulevard was lined with people waiting for the parade to start. The high school marching band was standing in forma-tion, ready to go. Mayor Lodge was sitting in a con-vertible with the president of the Sweet Valley

Historical Society. At the end of the street, the parade floats were lined up and waiting.

"There's the citizenship float!" Jessica exclaimed.

"Ooh, it's beautiful!" Elizabeth cried.

The float was designed to look like old-time Sweet Valley, with real grass and trees and a plaster horse and cow. The sides were decorated with flowers and ribbons. A sign across each side read SWEET VALLEY PUBLIC SCHOOLS PRESENT THE JUNIOR CITIZENS OF THE YEAR!

"Look, there's Janet and Kimberly!" Jessica said. Kimberly Haver had won the election for seventh-grade Citizen of the Year and Janet Howell had won for eighth-grade citizen. The girls were standing together on the float, looking proud and happy in their old-fashioned, flowing pioneer dresses.

"All the Citizens of the Year from the middle school are members of the Unicorns," Sandra said. She turned to Jessica. "That's a real honor for your club."

"If it weren't for you, there would only be two Unicorns up there," Jessica replied. "Thanks, Sandra."

Mr. Wakefield pulled into the parking lot reserved for people in the parade and parked the van. Jessica was so excited she could hardly sit still. Eagerly, she threw open her door and leapt out. She lifted her skirt so she wouldn't trip and ran toward the float as fast as she could.

"Wait for me!" she cried as she scrambled up the steps to join Janet and Kimberly.

"What are you doing here?" Janet asked. "What happened to Sandra?"

"It's a long story," Jessica said. "I'll tell you later. Right now I just want to enjoy myself."

The float started moving. Jessica looked down at the crowd. Everyone was cheering and waving. She smiled and waved back. She felt fantastic!

Two hours later, when the parade ended, Jessica climbed wearily off the citizenship float. Her legs hurt from standing up so long, her dress was pulling apart at the seams from waving so much, and her mouth was sore from smiling continuously. Still, she didn't mind. It had been a wonderful parade and she had loved every single minute of it.

Mr. and Mrs. Wakefield, Elizabeth, Steven, and Sandra were waiting to meet her at the end of the parade route. "You looked lovely," Mrs. Wakefield said, giving her daughter a kiss on the cheek.

"We're very proud of you, sweetheart," Mr. Wakefield added.

"I never could have done it without all of you," Jessica said generously. "Especially you, Sandra." She gave Sandra a hug. "Thanks for everything!"

* * *

Jessica woke up the next morning with a smile on her face. All night long she had dreamed about the Sweet Valley Days parade. What a thrill it had been to ride on the float with the whole town watching!

She jumped out of bed and started to get dressed. Then she noticed the remains of her pioneer dress hanging over a chair. Just looking at all the crooked buttons and ripped seams made her laugh.

She picked it up and looked at it. "What a mess!" she declared and then tossed it into her wastebasket. There was no way she could fix it. Next time she needed a dress for a special occasion, she was going to buy one, even if she had to spend her own money. It was bound to be a whole lot easier than making it. As far as she was concerned, her sewing career was over!

Jessica and Elizabeth spent the afternoon doing their homework so they could watch *Gone With the Wind* on television that night. They had seen the movie six times before. It was one of their all-time favorites.

"I just love all the dresses Vivien Leigh wears. And Clark Gable is so handsome," Jessica said dreamily.

Elizabeth nodded. "And the acting is so good," she said.

"Yes," Jessica agreed. "I bet I could be as great an

actress, though. Remember how wonderful I was in the school musical?" she reminded her sister.

"You were good, Jess. But you would have to study for years before you got a great role like this one," Elizabeth said sensibly.

"That's what you think!" Jessica exclaimed. She watched the television screen and recited the lines along with the actress.

"Sounds like Scarlett O'Hara has an echo," Elizabeth joked.

"Ha ha," Jessica replied. "Just wait, Lizzie. I'm going to be a great actress one day. You'll see!"

Elizabeth smiled knowingly. How many times had Jessica started something that she never saw through to the end? Just yesterday she had wanted to be a clothing designer. Today she wanted to be a famous actress. It was true that her twin had a flair for the dramatic, but Elizabeth wouldn't believe a word Jessica said until she proved that it was true.

Is Jessica serious about becoming a famous actress? Find out in Sweet Valley Twins #32, **JESSICA ON STAGE.**

☐ **15669-1 TAKING CHARGE #26** **$2.75**
☐ **15681-0 TEAMWORK #27** **$2.75**
☐ **15688-8 APRIL FOOL! #28** **$2.75**
☐ **15695-0 JESSICA AND THE BRAT ATTACK #29 $2.75**
☐ **15715-9 PRINCESS ELIZABETH #30** **$2.75**